Sword

Sword

a novel by DA CHEN

LAURA GERINGER BOOKS

An Imprint of HarperCollins*Publishers*

Sword

Library of Congress Cataloging-in-Publication Data
Chen, Da, date
  Sword / a novel by Da Chen. — 1st ed.
    p. cm.
  Summary: When Miu Miu turns fifteen, she learns the truth about
her father's violent death and discovers that she must avenge his mur-
der before she can marry the man to whom she is betrothed. Based on
a story told to the author by a former prisoner during China's Cultural
Revolution.
  ISBN 978-0-06-144758-7 (trade bdg.)
  ISBN 978-0-06-144759-4 (lib. bdg.)
  [1. Revenge—Fiction. 2. China—Fiction.] I. Title. II. Series:
Forbidden Tales.
PZ7.C41815 2008   2008010774
[Fic]—dc22   CIP
                                                               AC

Typography by Jennifer Rozbruch
1 2 3 4 5 6 7 8 9 10
❖
First Edition

To Al Roker,
Maker of blue skies
Champion of Quills Award

Prologue

AR KIN WAS the first ex-convict I had ever met. He was arrested for openly criticizing the Communist Party and sent to Xinjiang province, which was China's Siberia. The whole town thought they had seen the last of him, since nobody ever returned from there alive; so did his wife, who was forced to sign a divorce paper and later married another man. To the surprise of everyone in our village, Ar Kin showed up at her door after serving his full twenty-year sentence.

Rumor had it that he spent his years imprisoned in a labor camp, digging the side of a mountain. He was no longer the handsome young man they said he had been. His back was hunched and his hair had turned white. But his eyes still gleamed with intelligence.

His ex-wife, who did not even recognize him at first, refused to take him back. She had a new family; even his two kids had assumed their stepfather's surname and viewed that man as their father. So Ar Kin gathered his stuff and, with the money he had saved from his twenty years of hard labor (convicts were paid a little for their work), built a two-room cottage on a narrow dirt road midway between the woods and the Dong Jing River. He lived there by himself, and the townspeople thought it fitting that a social outcast reside at the edge of town, for it gave them the comfort of distance. He was treated like a lunatic or a leper, and rumors always seemed to swirl around him. It was whispered that a younger woman was sometimes seen going to his hut late at night; some guessed her to be a pretty widow from the next town. He supposedly ate grilled meat like a northern nomad, chewed his tea leaves, and ate peppers that would burn your throat like fire. He became a fleeting shadow, never venturing out of his hut during the day.

Once I took my friends Buckle, Jie, and Ciang and walked the narrow, muddy dirt road to the graveyard near Ar Kin's house, where we pretended to play around the tombstones. When we saw no trace of him inside the hut, we crawled to the windows and strained our necks for a glimpse of the inside. The two rooms were as clean and neat as an army barracks. There was no bed, just a huge rug with animal fur on top. Though I had never seen one before, I had no doubt that it was a tiger hide he had brought home from up north. The furniture in the living room was short-legged, in the northern style, and he had adopted the northerners' custom of sitting and sleeping on the floor.

Ar Kin became the object of great speculation and curiosity. Even the leaders of the commune whispered about him. It was as if the twenty years of hard labor had forever branded him a criminal beyond redemption. The leaders left him alone to do as he pleased.

An old man rejected by society and abandoned by his own family, he had hit the bottom—no one could sink any lower than that. But in his few public appearances, Ar Kin seemed carefree and untroubled, even content. No one knew where he got all the money to put fish, meat, good tobacco, and liquor on his table. And then there were those great books he was rumored to possess. They said he had dumped most of his belongings on his way home from prison, and all of what he had carried with him was in two huge sacks—rare forbidden books of legends, romances, war stories, mysteries, and fairy tales. I wanted to see where he kept them, but each time we sniffed around his dirt hut, he always showed up mysteriously behind us, staring at us silently until we ran off, scared.

Soon people began to drop by his cottage to chat, have a smoke, and drink tea with him. He never seemed to have to work, yet he kept an endless supply of tea and tobacco for his guests, old and young. In those days it was not uncommon for some poor smokers and tea drinkers to live on others' supplies. Such people would come to his house to chop wood, clean the house, and run errands for him.

No one knew at what point or why the people of Yellow Stone began to forget who he was and started treating Ar Kin like a person of importance. Maybe it was the day the leader of the labor brigade dropped by and had tea with him. Or maybe it was the day the fat deputy chief of the commune had his first Western cigar at the humble cottage and left with a bottle of rare rice wine. Perhaps it was Ar Kin's exotic stories about the faraway labor camp and the other inmates, strange and talented characters, that won people over. Or maybe it was just his magnetism.

Many nights I filled my spare time by squeezing into his doorway and claiming a spot on the crowded floor, listening devotedly to his tales of another time and place, after enduring a few slaps on the head from the older folks who didn't want me there. He was an optimist, and his words made you see the bright colors of spring and the majestic snow-capped mountains of Xinjiang. The sunsets in his tales were especially glorious, and the people with whom he had shared his life the most gifted. We grew to know his roommate at the labor camp, a violinist from the big city of Shanghai, who was still there digging the snow, and the moody poet who spoke his poems aloud only in his dreams in the quiet of night.

In Ar Kin's slow and casual way of speaking, life in the miserable labor camp was transformed into story filled with colorful characters and beautiful scenery. I laughed and cried over his stories and would lie in bed thinking of those tales long after the lanterns were blown out.

On cold winter nights we gathered about him, listening to him speak as he sat at the short tea table in the middle of the room. On muggy summer nights we would sit around the newly dug well, hanging on to every detail of his tales as if they were the sweetest breeze from the Pacific. There were toothless old men, graying middle-aged ones, young fathers with little babies in their arms, nursing mothers, and starry-eyed children like me. Ar Kin's tales opened our minds to a world outside our village—a world unknown to us. He took us on a journey as we sat back in his comfortable chairs, letting him fill our hungry minds with endless wisdom and humor.

As I grew older, I began to realize it was not his sharp wit but his spirit that had survived the coldest of winters, drawing us to him like a bright star. His love of life was so infectious, it made me wish I had been there with him as he got up every morning in darkness and climbed the icy mountain. Warmth came out of those bitter stories. He taught us that one could live a happy life in total misery—that happiness came from within.

His was the only place where lantern light still shone after midnight in the whole town of Yellow Stone. I don't know how else I would have idled away those long evenings. And the best nights were when I was sitting right next to Ar Kin.

On one such evening Ar Kin told us that on the day of his release from the labor camp, one of his best friends, a fellow prisoner, gave him an address. His friend said he would give Ar Kin his books if he was willing to make the journey to the man's hometown in the mountains near Fujian province. Ar Kin made the trip and paid a few porters to transport the books safely, dodging several checkpoints along the way where soldiers from the Red Army would have confiscated and burned them.

After he had gradually become accepted by the villagers, Ar Kin opened a book renting business out of his home. Ostensibly he rented only the good books that praised the revolutionary heroism of China's Communist Party. But it was his not-so-secret, forbidden collection of fiction that people really wanted. Some books stayed on the waiting list for months, like *Strange Stories from Liaozhai* and *Shui Hu Zhuan*—Outlaws of the Marsh.

During the Cultural Revolution, when all commercial publications were shut down and all the old literature burned and public libraries closed, Ar Kin's bookstore was heaven on earth. I had to collect two allowances, one from Dad and another from Grandpa, in order to rent the many books I read at Ar Kin's.

My juiciest Saturday afternoons were there, sitting on a stool in the corner of the room with my pile of ten picture books, forgetting about the rest of the world. The most perfect times were when it was raining hard outside, with the music of raindrops beating the surface of the river nearby. With peace and tranquility and a book in hand, I would glide into a magical world, staying there until I could no longer hold my pee or I got so hungry that I couldn't read anymore. Some books were so good, I rented them five times. I even brought my friends Buckle, Ciang, and Jie to read with me on the afternoons Ar Kin was in a good mood.

My favorites were the Monkey King stories, in which the monkey could change colors and shape at will, and appear in any form. He was loyal to his master, a Buddhist monk who was making the long trip to the west to seek truth. There were other war books and romances, but none captured my imagination as much as the Monkey King did.

One day I overheard a town cadre, a public official, tell his friend that Ar Kin was running a risky business, and if he wasn't careful, he would end up in prison once more when the next political movement came along. Soon afterward my parents began to check my school bags for the rented books and whispered to me that no more forbidden books were to be brought home. I felt cheated—and scared. I could tell that another political purge was on its way when my parents became nervous and began whispering. It was time to kill another chicken to scare the monkey, as the saying went. But who would it be?

Late one night we were awakened by whistling, shouting, and screaming. There was a fire at the edge of town; I could see the distant flames from my window. My heart sank when they told me that it was Ar Kin's home on fire.

As his books burned, the heat and flames carried the ashes high into the black sky. His neighbors passed buckets of water drawn from the nearby river to quench the fire, but it was the dry season. A west wind fueled the fire, and the little cottage burned to the ground.

The next morning I went to his house with the other children and joined the large crowd looking on from a distance. The ground was covered with dark ash, as if a black rain had washed down upon it. Ar Kin sat on a rock, alone, smoking his pipe and staring into the sky.

I dreamed of those books that night and

many nights after the fire, feeling a deep loss. Even in the predawn quiet of New York's Hudson Valley, I still sometimes dream of my small hometown village in China and remember Ar Kin and the many stories he told.

What follows is a tale that he told many years ago, many thousands of miles away. The story of a sword and a brave girl named Miu Miu.

One 劍

ON THE MORNING of Miu Miu's fifteenth birthday, her mother did not arrange a visit by a matchmaker, as all the mothers of Goose Village did when their daughters reached marriageable age. Instead, Miu Miu rose early to pick a basketful of green olives from the cliff of Goose Mountain behind her village. She washed them clean in the gurgling river fronting the town's houses and laid the olives, a symbol of longevity, before her father's memorial name plaque placed in the ancestral hall on the sacred central hearth in their two-story brick home. The delicate wooden plaque was mounted on a wide bronze base, with her father's name engraved at the top and the dates of his birth and death at the bottom. It was always there, standing solemnly, reminding Miu Miu every day that even though Father had died before she was born, he was always there, watching over her, no matter that he was no longer among the living. Sometimes she thought the only proof of his having lived was this evidence of his death.

Miu Miu prayed to Father every day, the first time at sunrise before she left the house for Goose Mountain to cut wood for her mother to sell in the market square, the second time at night just before crawling into bed after washing her face and feet, and combing her long dark hair.

She prayed for Father's spirit to accompany Mother so that she would not be so sad and lonely, tormented by his absence. And she prayed for the day that Father's ghost would be lifted up by Buddha to ascend to Heaven from the hellish dungeon where all the dead languished before going anywhere. She never begged anything from Father for herself, for she did not need anything. She felt whole as an egg, round and lively, sufficient unto herself. God had given her a sturdy body and a steely mind. She saw the absence of a living father as a mark of fate, like rocks jutting up in a river's path, or dark moles on smooth skin: It was something to bear, something to endure, nothing more.

But today, on this very first day of her adult life, an occasion that other households of means would mark with much celebration honoring the end of girlhood and the coming of womanhood, Miu Miu's heart felt hollow. Her mind longed for something, though what that was she did not know. All she knew was that the canons of the Miu clan and the customs of Goose Village dictated that a girl turning fifteen be visited by a matchmaker, who would appear at her door as though unforeseen, bright and early, dressed in red, with a wild bloom pinned to her head. The mother of the household would wear red as well, and welcome the guest, pretending to be surprised by her visit. The matchmaker—the messenger of love, the ambassador of happiness—would bow and shout the girl's name in a joyful voice, and the father of the household would appear, dressed in a long red silk gown, clasping his hands together, offering deep and grateful bows. The matchmaker, usually a hunched woman of about fifty with crooked fingers, would roll her oily tongue and say, as she always did, "Don't thank me. Thank Yue Lao, the moon deity, and only do so after I show you whom I've got up my sleeve."

The mother would pull out a chair in the central hall, already deftly arranged in the traditional square of four, and invite the matchmaker to sit. The father would pour the first cup of tea while the mother rushed to the blushing daughter's *xiu fang* (bedroom) and dragged her down to join the early guest, who would then pull out a strip of red silk from within her left sleeve, inscribed with names of possible grooms. As long as the shy but beaming daughter was nodding, the matchmaker would keep reading off her silk list, one suitor after another. The wedding fee would be extracted from the groom's coffers, and the age, health, and appearance of the man were never objects of discussion unless the suitor was of little means.

But such a scene did not occur on the dreary birthday morning when Miu Miu turned fifteen. Of course, there was no possibility of her mother wearing red. Widows of Goose Village and beyond could wear only black until their own deaths. Red was the hue of the married sisters of the village who still had their husbands around, even though their husbands might be shared with other wives and concubines in *da fang* and *xiao fang*s—the big bedroom and smaller bedrooms.

There didn't seem to be a hint of any surprises coming Miu Miu's way, this day or the next, not in this life, for even if a matchmaker did show up, Miu Miu would stick to her childhood pledge to remain by her mother's side, protecting her till the end of her days.

The hens gargled as they did every morning, announcing the laying of their eggs, warm in their straw nests. Cocky roosters charged after them, their heads and tails lowered, vying for another round of early coupling. The peach trees in the front yard sang if you listened carefully to the breeze blowing along Goose River, passing through Goose Valley each morning along various paths, depending on which way the wind blew: from east to west, it whispered; north to south, it shouted, blending with the yawns of villagers waking, cows mooing, mountain goats baying, and the geese—a village full of them—honking noisily.

The cause of such sound and fury could only be blamed on her mother. All things seemed to revolve around Miu Miu's mother, the mistress of their humble manor. Hens seemed to lay eggs just for her. If Miu Miu tried to gather their morning eggs, the hens would peck her hands bloody with their pointy beaks, and the roosters would erect their combs, stretch their wings, and fluff up their feathers as if confronting a duelist. But for Mother the hens clucked proudly, reporting their production, and the roosters charged playfully after Mother's heels in hopes of receiving their morning feed.

This morning, however, Mother was holding a jar of yellow wine. "What are you praying for?" she asked, as Miu Miu bowed before Father's plaque.

"I am thanking him for giving me life."

"The olives are too green, and your thanks are empty," Mother said, her voice cold. She slammed the sturdy wine jar on the table so hard that it caused Father's plaque to fall on its face.

"Mother!" Reaching over, Miu Miu hurriedly set the name plaque upright again.

"It is only hollow wood that will rot with years and crumble with time."

"Then what isn't hollow?"

"Your father's dying wish!" Mother said sternly. "He pledged you to the son of his apprentice, the bearer of a necklace matching this one." Mother fished out a jade necklace from inside her left sleeve pocket and hung it over Miu Miu's neck.

Miu Miu pinched the jade with her fingers and examined its engravings. On the face was carved, in an archaic style of calligraphy, the name Tong Ting. On the back was a tiger, which must be the zodiac sign of his birth. The jade was of the palest blue. "What is his name?"

"Tong Ting of Cicada Village," Mother said, adjusting the necklace.

"Is he coming to claim me today?" Miu Miu asked, blushing now.

"No, not yet."

"Why not?"

"He is waiting for our request."

"Isn't it the custom for the man's family to initiate the ritual?"

"It is." Mother combed her fingers through Miu Miu's hair. "But this is no customary betrothal. Once the request is proffered in the manner prescribed in your father's will—by a letter bearing the red prints of your left palm and my right—the match is to be made. But Tong Ting cannot claim you as his bride until he fulfills the pledge imposed by our village elder." Mother lowered her eyes.

"What is that pledge?" Miu Miu prompted.

"To avenge Father."

"Avenge?" Miu Miu was shocked. "Didn't Father drown?"

Silently Mother poured the yellow wine into two little cups and placed them before Father's plaque. It had been his favorite liquor, with the bitter taste of ginseng and black barley, the kind he drank every night—two little cups before going to bed, to chase away the chill. Like the other villagers, Mother believed that the wine had power to call upon the dead who still hovered in the form of spirits. After much kowtowing to them, the lingering spirits would be able to share in the blessings of the wine as it flowed from the living to the dead through an invisible bridge connecting this earth to the netherworld.

On such wine-sharing occasions, Mother would usually wear a red bloom in her hair—the only touch of red she secretly allowed herself—and blush like a shy bride, as if she were indeed in the company of her husband. There would be a certain nervous cheerfulness in her demeanor. But not today. Dark circles ringed her almond-shaped eyes, and she did not kneel beside Miu Miu as she usually did, pouring the wine. Nor did she weep. In a sudden, fierce movement, Mother pounded the desk, making the two little cups jump, spilling some of the yellow wine.

"Mother, what is the matter?"

There was a dazed look in Mother's eyes as they fixed on Father's plaque.

"How did Father die?" Miu Miu asked, much disturbed.

"A vile death," Mother said, sinking down

into an armchair with her hands clasped, her fingers twisting together, pain and sorrow etched on her face. "You only know your father to be a swordmaker. What you do not know is that he was a legendary *dao xian*, one unmatched in his generation. He was celebrated by all men of arms, rich and poor alike. His swords were delicate and fierce, deft and deadly. But your father made all his patrons pledge one thing."

"What was that?"

"That they would kill only for justice, never for greed; that they would fight for peace. He was a thinker, full of hope. Most of his swords were kept on display, symbols of the grand tradition of swordmaking. They hung on the walls of the dukes and earls of this kingdom, of noble generals, and warriors of yesteryear, as a reminder of their fighting days and the glory of their battles.

"Miu swords were a badge of honor to celebrate a life of battle and the life of a patriot or a peacemaker. Some believed that your father's swords attained the rank of *shen ping*, spirit treasures capable of doing magical wonders, such as defending their owners when the kindred souls of sword and owner merged, much the same way a horse salvages his fallen rider's life by dragging him to safety.

"Your father was modest. He refused to believe in such things. He was always the first to deny any such claim, and was so offended by those rumors that he once bought back a sword from its owner at twice the price, simply to stop the rumors." Mother picked up a small cup of wine and took a deep sip. The bitter taste of the wine made her shiver.

"One day in the third year of Emperor Ching's reign," she continued, "his favorite concubine was rumored to have given birth. Not to a prince or a princess but to a soft pouch containing a chunk of iron, much to the emperor's dismay. Legions of doctors were called upon and consulted. So were gemstone and metal experts. None could offer any satisfactory explanation.

"The emperor was displeased until an itinerant fortune-teller prophesied, with the help of a court astrologer and geomancer, that the iron was a rare gift from Heaven delivered through the medium of his concubine's womb to aid the emperor in his earthly conquest. Thus, he must seek the finest swordsmith to mold this metal into the fiercest weapon—a treasure blessed with heavenly magic, which would forever defend him.

"I still remember the morning when the village road suddenly trembled with scores of horses' hooves. One could see the dust rising miles ahead of the emperor's men, proclaiming their coming. It was a day of joy and sadness. The emperor had given his mandate that your father be the swordsmith to make such a weapon out of the heavenly ore. And though your father received this honor with much misgiving, he dove into the sacred commission with great dedication.

"For the next three months, he hammered away at the precious metal, slowly shaping the formless metal into the handsomest sword. When Father struck his hammer the last time at the stroke of midnight on one June day and carved his signature onto the handle, the sword, as if delighted by its birth, gave off a brilliant light that filled his workshop and shone through the skylight, fanning into the Heaven to brighten a corner of the night sky. It was no ordinary light but an eerie, pure, blood-red hue, confirming its rare origin. It was a sign of unimaginable power and unparalleled strength.

"The emperor demanded that Father deliver the sword himself to the royal palace. A hundred of the emperor's guards and a general accompanied him. Father, a swordsmith to the bone, should have been proud, but upon leaving for the palace, he was despondent. He knelt before me and leaned his head against my swollen belly, six months ripe with you. Tears flowed down his cheeks. 'I have a premonition that this honor will bring tragedy to our family,' he told me. Then he said that he might never come home again . . . and he never did."

Mother took another deep sip from the wine cup.

"But why?"

"The emperor feared that your father might make another sword that would match the magic of the one belonging to him, or even surpass it. His counselors had also whispered poison in his ears, accusing your father of aiding and abetting rioting bandits and dissenting warlords. The emperor had your father's eyeballs gouged out so that he could not see again. He had his tongue cut to its root so that your father could speak no more. He had his hands cut off at the wrists so that he could never make another sword for good or evil, and his feet chopped off so that he could not escape. Then he had him thrown into a manure hole to languish for days before he finally drowned in filth."

"Father!" Miu Miu felt her cheeks burn with the fire of rage, her heart pounding so that she could barely breathe. Overwhelmed by the gruesome images in her mind, she burst into sobs so deep, they rocked her to the very bottom of her soul.

Mother held her in her arms. When the sobbing ceased, Mother passed her the yellow wine. Receiving it with shaking hands, Miu Miu tossed it back, letting the bitterness burn down her throat. Bitterness was what she needed. It numbed her nerves and calmed her pulses. But it did not touch the deep sadness that had taken root in her as she gazed at Father's name plaque through a veil of tears. She used to see a tall, handsome man there in the plaque, smiling contentedly, greeting her warmly each morning as she prayed to him. Now all she saw in her mind's eye was a footless, handless horror with eyeless sockets and a bleeding tongue stump, trying to call out to her.

She struck her forehead down on the hard floor again and again in respectful kowtows, tears gushing from her eyes.

"I told you your father's true story because today is the day that you become a woman,"

Mother said. "Today is the day you swear to avenge your father by sending our request to the boy named Tong Ting, and by doing your part: agreeing to marry a boy you have never met, a man who will likely never make it back from this act of vengeance; the husband who will widow you as your father did me."

Miu Miu's chest heaved now with mournful emotions she had never known existed and the crushing weight of a pledge. "Why make an innocent man pay what he does not owe? Why send this stranger to his certain death? Why can't I go instead to right the wrong done to Father, to us, to the name of Miu?"

"No." Mother shook her head.

"Have I not been cutting the trees like a young man?" Miu Miu asked. "Have I not been carrying heavy sacks of rice on my shoulders? Haven't you always called me boyish?"

"I've heard enough."

Though quick-minded and able, Miu Miu had never been deft at the tasks of embroidery, making dumplings, or shoe stitching—girlish chores Mother had wanted her to excel in so that she would make a good wife. Miu Miu had once broken the ancestral needle Mother had inherited from her grandma, who in turn had received it from *her* own mother. It was a sign, Mother had said: Something in the chain of inheritance had been broken. But Miu Miu didn't believe in such things as omens and curses; she believed in the things that were reliable, like the rising of the sun and the shining of the moon.

Mother's hands trembled. After a long moment, she said, "If you so choose, I will have to seek permission from the elder. What a miserable man," she added bitterly. "When the emperor's envoys came to Goose Village, our obsequious elder was the first to run to the bridge to kneel in welcome, inviting the envoys to dine at his home, claiming that your father and I were named as his first cousins in his generational chronicle. He even asked your father to beg on his behalf for an official appointment from the royal court. But he was the quickest to spit on me after your father's death, and the first to turn on me when your father was accused of being a rebel and I was implicated as his wife. I was watched over by the elder's men so that when the royal guards arrived, the elder would not be implicated. Fortunately the palace did not know of my pregnancy with you, or they would have been here sooner. By the time they came to our door, I was beyond their reach."

"How?"

"Our village monk dispatched a young apprentice from the temple to escort me, disguised as a man, to seek protection at Yu Mei Mountain Nunnery. The abbess kindly took me in. Under their roof you were born and by the nuns' hands were you raised. Oh, how they adored you." Tears trailed down Mother's cheeks. "Before you even learned to walk, you could clasp your little hands and perform perfect kowtows. Your first words were prayers, your first song that of a chant. Oh, what heavenly souls they were. When we departed, the abbess gave you that old hand mirror on your dresser, so that you could see your hair, shaven at birth, grow back, bit by bit, day by day." Pausing, she slowly raised both hands to peel a wig off her scalp. "They burned the roots of all my hair, so as not to raise the suspicion of visitors or the emperor's garrison."

"Mother!" Miu Miu gasped, shocked at her mother's baldness. She covered her mouth with trembling hands. "All these years. How did you manage to hide it from everyone?"

"By seldom taking this hairpiece off. And by not letting you play with my hair, and washing it only when you are far away in the mountains. On bathing days, I would trail you until you disappeared into the woods." She moved to put her wig back on.

"Not yet." Miu Miu stilled Mother's hands and studied her carefully before letting her don the wig once more. "Mother, you would have been a beautiful nun."

Mother smiled sadly. "When we returned, the elder demanded that the revenge pledge be forced on your betrothed. Our village had suffered much: three men were beheaded, bringing even more shame to the village."

"I've heard enough, Mother. What must I do now?"

"The emperor must be killed with your father's female sword. Knowing that his days were numbered when he was called upon to make the emperor's sword, your father fashioned a second sword, an even more vibrant female one from that same chunk of iron, stronger than the male sword he made for the emperor, so that we could take on his murderer. Here." Mother pushed aside the desk upon which Father's memorial plaque stood, and removed a handwoven straw rug from the floor. "Dig it up here. Three feet down, and you will find it."

Miu Miu ran to the work shed and returned with a sharp hoe. She struck the surface hard, breaking a brick, and dug into the earth beneath. Mud flew and more bricks broke before Mother slowed her down and Miu Miu saw the lid of a wooden box.

"Careful now," Mother admonished. Bending down, she gently lifted out the box, dusting off the soil with her sleeves. The exterior of the box was roughly hewn, but the interior was all silk and satin wrapping the sword, as if it were not a tool of blood and battle but a fragile infant, freshly born, needing all the gentleness you could give it. Unsheathed, the sword lay brilliant in Mother's hands, slender and delicate, gleaming in the morning sun that filtered in through the window. It gave off a glint of light blue, as if it were a slice of autumnal sky, as if it had just been minted, not a day old or an hour aged, fresh from its maker.

Miu Miu had seen many swords made by Father; some still hung on the walls of his workshop, others she had used in her daily practices; still more were too heavy for her arms and too clumsy for her grip. But this one seemed a perfect fit for her with its long, thin blade—light but with a fierce edge. She felt a strangely tender desire for it, a wish to care for it always, as she reached out her hands.

"Such a sword cannot be held without the blessing of its maker first," Mother said sternly.

For the third time that morning Miu Miu knelt piously and paid her respects to her father with three deep kowtows before his plaque. Only then did Mother place the sword in her waiting hands.

Miu Miu closed her eyes, wanting the moment to be silent and calm, sacred and pious. It was a moment she had long awaited without knowing it: a moment to touch Father's hands; a moment when his blood and hers merged.

Two 劍

LATE THAT NIGHT, Mother returned home after pleading on Miu Miu's behalf with the elder. When she said quietly, "You are beholden to the same honor as a son now," Miu Miu knelt and kissed her dry hand.

Mother walked to an old trunk that had always been locked. Dusting off the lid, she unlocked it with a rusty key. The old trunk yielded, revealing the contents it had been hoarding: Father's old clothes. Fetching out a blue robe, Mother held it against Miu Miu's shoulders. "This will fit you well with a few trims and stitches."

"Am I to wear this?" Miu Miu asked.

"You are a son now. The daughter that you were is dead." Mother's lips quivered. "A widow has few choices; a widow's daughter even less." Mother went into the next room and returned with a sewing box containing scissors big and small, needles thin and thick, and threads, coiled and rolled. She laid Father's robe flat on a square table and smoothed its wrinkles with her fingers. Decisively, she cut open its flanks, nipped a few inches away; pinched the shoulders, narrowing them; and opened the sleeves at the seams before taking in both their width and length. She cut off a foot of material from the bottom hem.

Silently, Miu Miu watched as Mother deftly sewed all the robe's portions back together. Hours later, Mother bit off the end of the last thread and said, "Put this on." Miu Miu did and found that it fit perfectly after another inch was trimmed from the bottom hem.

Mother put Father's old hat on Miu Miu's head and nodded in satisfaction. "Now you are a man" was all Mother said. Urging Miu Miu to bed, she blew out the lantern.

Miu Miu lay on their bed next to her mother, holding her from behind, the same way Mother used to cuddle her on cold winter nights when she was a little girl. She lay awake until midnight, then dozed off only to be woken by Mother's long sighs and quiet sobs.

At first light Mother got up, insisting on performing the village *chu jia* farewell ritual by washing Miu Miu's hands and face with mint water and combing her hair one last time. Mother was able to hold back her tears then, but when Miu Miu returned the favor by performing the *xie lau* ritual of thanking the old, by offering a cup of freshly brewed tea as she knelt and kowtowed, Mother burst once more into sobs. She knocked the teacup away, breaking it to pieces on the ground. "One to die young, the other to live old and bitter. What a cursed fate!"

"I won't die. I'll be back to care for you until your last days of life," Miu Miu told her.

"No more promises or pledges. Remember who you are and what you must do. Leave now and go far. Your father has brought you this curse; he will help you in your need. He is with you in spirit, your guiding star. In all this there is blessing, though a curse it all seems to be. Go!" She pushed Miu Miu out the door.

Bidding her mother good-bye, Miu Miu touched and rattled her bamboo name stick hanging on the front door next to her mother's and started on the journey to Chang'an, the capital city of the Tang Dynasty.

A neighbor who passed by on his mule, loaded down with morning vegetables, did not recognize Miu Miu. He nodded to her the way one man would to another man. The other mule men, who always greeted her each morning on her way to the mountains to cut trees, simply ignored her as some stranger on the road.

Miu Miu was pleased: Her disguise was a

success. She bounced with a manly gait, swinging from side to side rather than moving with the gingerly silkworm walk that Mother had often urged upon her, which required taking tiny steps, moving just her feet, minimizing movement in her knees and hips. The thought of that walk, known poetically as "three inches of golden lotus," prompted her to swing her steps even wider now. She felt a great elation with such carefree strides, and the freedom of her baggy robe that flopped as she stomped down the dusty morning path toward Chang'an.

Three

THE GRASSY ROAD widened as Miu Miu left Goose Village. Southbound itinerants yawned, letting their sleepy feet fumble ahead. Northbound merchants dozed off spinelessly like bending willow twigs as they rode on their mules, trotting to the early market to sell hay. The honking of Goose Village faded the farther north she strode. The village's looming pagoda disappeared from view in the mist, and the smell of horse and mule manure replaced the smell of goose droppings.

When she came to a bend in the trail, Miu Miu dashed onto a narrow footpath where the grass had not been beaten down, full of leaping frogs, hidden crickets, and baby snakes. Men might make the roads, but other creatures guarded them: That was the rule of the road, not just of Goose Village, but everywhere.

The road to Chang'an had no shortcut, and neither did Miu Miu's destiny. The main path was known as the Big Post Road. Six yards wide and straight as a needle, it pulled and stitched through wrinkly villages and unwilling townships all the way up north.

Miu Miu wondered if the Big Post Road had been built first to encourage the growth of villages, or if the villages had been there first, awaiting and necessitating the road. If the latter, why was the road straight, unlike other roads and footpaths Miu Miu knew? Maybe it wasn't really straight, only thought to be so by those journeying up or down its wide path. Miles and miles of mindless wandering could flatten your feet and deceive your eyes if you kept looking ahead and yearning for home, your heart full of hope, flying straight like a quick arrow.

As she branched off the main road, Miu Miu noticed some merchants of the road looking her way, perhaps thinking that she was taking a break or needed to relieve herself by the roadside. But Miu Miu wasn't taking a leak or resting her feet, at least not for now. She had one last secret farewell—girlhood was an urn full of secrets. Secrets and hidden shames. On the Crimson Day of her fourteenth year, Miu Miu had felt the sudden churning of her guts just before a trickle of blood smeared the saddle of the pony she was riding and dripped down the white beast's sunken flanks. She had waded into a secluded cove to wash herself clean, squatting naked in the gurgling brook. Redness stained the water, then thinned away, swirling downstream.

That very day, Mother had boiled her two round chicken eggs and painted them red with *yinzi*, the crushed bloom of a garden tree: one male egg, the other female, chosen by holding them up against a bright sun. Male eggs enclosed just a yoke, while female eggs were threaded with tiny arteries and veins. Mother had extolled Miu Miu's fertility and rejoiced in that distant promise of continuity.

Miu Miu had thought much and often of that day, during her mountain climbs or valley treks, not just to busy her head and lessen the weight on her back and slanting shoulders, but to think her life through—a life unlike that of a hen, whose chore was merely to lay eggs and daily face the bullying of roosters and sometimes even geese. How Miu Miu wished, each time she saw the backyard hens being harassed by the roosters, that they would defy the males the same way they chased after an egg thief—with heads low, eyes mean, and wings paddling.

Those laughable roosters, spiteful and wanton. When they were after a hen, they would sometimes run through a bonfire, setting their feathers aflame, or try to fly over a river and, misjudging their reach, fall into the churning water. Miu Miu had seen one drowned in such a way, becoming perhaps a dinner for six or a soup for twelve for the downriver folks who salvaged him. They said it was not the rooster's doing that had undone him: The hens were to blame for igniting his lust.

Miu Miu was certain that it was not mutual love that had maddened that rooster to his fateful flight. Had it been so, the hen would not have been trembling and squatting on the ground, as if seeing an eagle of death coming for her. It had been no love, merely feathery madness. She'd always wondered if that fate was to befall her. She knew for certain that she did not want to be a human hen. Miu Miu was no hen. The day was still young, she had just turned fifteen, and vengeance was waiting.

Last night, after Mother finally fell asleep beside her, Miu Miu had indulged in a brief reprieve from the anxieties of her pending trip, fantasizing in that bed with the stars unblinking and a lone moon shining above.

She had dreamed of him, a man she had never known existed: Tong Ting of Cicada Village. How had he existed for so long without her ever knowing?

She didn't dream of anything in particular about him. She only dreamed of being claimed, being desired by virtue of passion and not right of possession, by that boy far away. He was hers now, only by virtue of a pledge. But he was hers nonetheless.

Mother had shown her earlier how the boy's name was written; there were numerous phonetic cousins to confuse one to no end in the Chinese language. His name, she said, meant "vast pavilion," one that Miu Miu imagined perched atop a steep cliff, facing a calm sea veiled behind a lingering mist where wine-sipping poets spent lazy days shouting their poetry to one another in a *shi jing* poetry-matching contest.

In that brief moment of blushing and dreaming, Miu Miu imagined Tong Ting to be a man of vast heart, if not fortune, who stood tall, as his name suggested. But names were just names. You could not really know a man just by the advertisement of his fine-sounding name. Take the lazy-eyed goose farmer named Da Fu, which meant "mighty fortune," who possessed only three score geese, down from the five of his father's legacy and the seven of his grandpa's. Made desperate by his diminishing fortune, he often squeezed his mother geese to force eggs unwillingly out of them. Eventually fewer and fewer eggs came, so Da Fu snapped the birds' necks and boiled them to stave off his hunger, breaking the first rule of life in Goose Village: Never eat the goose that lays the eggs.

Then there was a man named Cheng En, which meant "inheriting grace," who was a manure thief, cursed by heredity with a humpback—a left-sided hump as big as a camel's. Villagers nicknamed him Cheng Shan, "inheriting the mountain"—a mountain of manure, that is. Hence, Tong Ting might turn out to be miserly little rat, a meek rabbit, or worse, a pampered mama's boy who whined all the time and still sucked his thumb. But why was she even thinking of him, now that her path was chosen? He would not wait around for her in a betrothal saddled with such hatred, stained with the blood of the last generation.

Accelerating to a run, Miu Miu thumped her feet across a narrow three-planked bridge spanning a quiet stream. The crude structure rattled violently as if in protest. Vengeance begot revenge, she thought, and hatred was perpetuated. She was the inheritor of her father's blood. What else could she ask of life, after all? She was a swordmaker's daughter.

A bamboo grove along a rising hill came into view, overgrown and shading an old, rickety temple with a red roof and forbidding walls. Some temples had nimble guard dogs; Goose Village Temple had a flock of white swans guarding it and grazing in its front yard, swimming in its two side ponds, and honking when strangers came their way. When petty thieves attempted to scale the walls, the swans chased after them like long-necked warriors. When a frequent guest like Miu Miu neared, they waddled up leisurely and cheerfully, gently pecking her robe, hoping for one of the tiny fish or frogs that Miu Miu often brought with her to feed them. But the mother swan of the little flock stood far back, aloof, a head taller than the others. She was the calm one. How she came to be that way, Wan Shan, the head monk here, had never told Miu Miu. Mother Swan was more reserved than usual, as if she intuited a difference in Miu Miu.

Fishing out a round rice cake from her backpack, Miu Miu tore it into sticky bits and pieces, which she scattered to the young and eager swans. The feeding freed her from their circling. As she came near Mother Swan, Miu Miu dipped her head down in a morning bow. The webfooted matriarch received this daily ritual like an empress, with her head high.

For the last seven years, Miu Miu had stopped here first every morning to take lessons in *wu shu*, the art of the warrior. Wan

Shan had been teaching her in secrecy inside the inner courtyard, skills ranging from *tie sha zhang* ("Iron Fists") to *bei ti* ("Northern Kicks") and *zhong yuan jiao* ("Central Kingdom Foot Rooting"). No martial artists of repute anywhere desired to make known their pupils, who were the keepers of their masters' secrets. When their identity was known, such seedlings were often uprooted and their branches ruthlessly cut down.

Miu Miu had once asked Master Wan why he had offered to tutor her without compensation. By way of reply, he showed her a sword wrapped in three layers of silk and satin, hidden below the floor of his cellar, where jars of yellow wine were kept and incense stacked.

Today he would still be waiting, sitting on the severed tree root where he always meditated with his eyes shut, preparing for Miu Miu's lesson. Today Miu Miu would silently go away to fulfill her destiny, and he would understand, for that had been the reason prompting this tutelage. It was all clear and simple now to Miu Miu.

Folding the note she had addressed to the monk, Miu Miu tried to feed it into Mother Swan's beak, the usual means of message sending for those familiar with the temple rules. But the old swan clenched her beak tightly shut. Miu Miu tried to entice her with a piece of rice cake she had kept for that purpose, but the beak remained stubbornly closed, leaving Miu Miu no choice but to break off one of the supple vines crawling over the temple wall and tie her note around Mother Swan's neck. The swan didn't like her vine collar a bit and tried to shake it off, but it remained fastened. Turning, she waddled slowly up the steps toward the temple gate.

Miu Miu smiled thankfully and struck her forehead on the dusty ground in three big kowtows of silent gratitude. A warrior's words were few, preferably none. Lingering farewells were for poets. And teary good-byes were for fearful brides facing an unknown life ahead. The soul of a warrior was pure like the water in a clear forest pond, their acts as natural as an autumn leaf falling in the wind. Farewells were not necessary in kung fu. A warrior's parting wasn't a parting. It was a separation to gain a new unity.

No *kung* (hardship) harvested, no *fu* (skill) gained.

Miu Miu had written the monk two succinct words: *jiu wu*—"overdue awareness." She had chosen a written good-bye over a face-to-face kowtow because it was a cardinal warrior's tenet that one sworn warrior share the other's plight, no matter the danger or hardship, even if it led to the earth's scorching heart. That was the fellowship of kung fu. She would not want this temple to be without its monk, the villagers without their guardian, or the swans without their master.

Miu Miu took one last glance at the temple, its tall pines, its whispering willows. Then off she ran as fast as could before her tears soiled the sacred ground.

"Farewell, Master Wan! I will make you

proud," she whispered.

Unbeknownst to her, a quick shadow leaped up into a tall pine, barely dipping the branches. And the monk's worried eyes followed her until she could be seen no more from inside the courtyard.

four 劍

BY DAY, MIU MIU traveled along the dusty road. When darkness came, she climbed into a big tree by the roadside and found herself a leafy branch to nest on for the night. She had always wanted to sleep in a tree, but Mother had never allowed her to spend the night outside, much less up in a tree. Now here she was with the ground beneath her and the sky hanging low above her like the roof of a cave.

Away from her home, from Mother, from Father's plaque, Miu Miu had never felt closer to all the things she held dear. She was her father's blood and her mother's pride. This was what she had been born to do, at all costs. Her heart was set.

On the third day of walking, Miu Miu arrived at Bridge Town. She found her tired feet slowing down and groggy eyes opening wide, marveling at the sudden vista. In the setting sun, the town seemed as if it were afloat, suspended upon a cobweb of crisscrossing rivulets and streams that dissected it into oddly shaped patches of streets and rickety homes, all bound together by the stitches of little stone bridges. A breeze was gently blowing from a gap between distant mountains, causing the green willow trees onshore to sway. Lotus blossoms drifted everywhere, pushed aside by the townsfolk rowing and poling their little wooden boats.

They don't need to move a toe to get around here, Miu Miu marveled, staring at her own toes, two of which peeked out from her torn boots. She had read about this magical place in a poem penned by a neighbor. He had called it an "earthly pearl."

Miu Miu picked up her gait, jogging joyfully toward Number One Bridge of Bridge Town, as the large red characters painted up on the bridge's headstone proudly proclaimed. The bridge was a stack of white stones, aged, with cracks visible along its span. Under it, a rocking boat was poled by a young man with beads of sweat on his chest and a shaven head. He sang as he pushed the boat with his dripping bamboo pole, pushing broad-leafed lotuses and their lovely blooms aside. To make perfect the blissful portrait, an old couple, clothed in expensive silk, sat in that rocking boat, holding hands as a young carp leaped up from the water, its flapping tail dispersing dragonflies and scaring away water birds perched on the lotus plants.

How Miu Miu wished she were that frolicking carp, ignorant of its tomorrow, or that dragonfly, frightened off one tender bloom only to alight upon another. Or even that smiling old couple, aged but undying, sure of their past if uncertain of their days yet to come.

She too was uncertain of her days, only certain that they were numbered.

Miu Miu turned to cross the long span of Number One Bridge.

"*Aiyah*, young man, you cannot pass yet," Miu Miu heard someone say. Turning, she found a dwarf standing next to her, dressed in a red robe. He stood a meager three feet tall, his head barely reaching Miu Miu's bound chest.

"Why are you stopping me?" Miu Miu asked, staring down at the dwarf.

"Are you blind? Didn't you see the sign?" the dwarf demanded. "Pay one yuan or you cannot cross Number One."

"I am not rich and have only little with me for a long journey. Can you let me through without the fee? One day I will repay you."

"No, I am not a usurer."

Miu Miu reached for her small pouch and pulled out all that she had: only three yuan. "I am sorry to have bothered you so," she said, sighing. "I can't afford to cross this bridge then. Can you kindly show me another way to Chang'an that bypasses your town?"

"I am no road guide to serve you and the many crossing my territory. You don't know who I am, do you?"

"No," said Miu Miu.

"I am the lord of Bridge Town. I have twenty tall wives, seventeen concubines, and fifty sons taller than I. I rule this town and the next three. All bridges are my possession. No one bargains with me, least of all you, a smelly southern boy of no distinction or honor."

"Mighty lord of bridges, I am doubly sorry that I have angered you. May I take my leave now and seek my own way around your territory?"

"No, you may not leave."

"Why not, my lord?"

"You have touched the stone of my bridge. You owe me the fee."

Miu Miu shook her money pouch, making

the coins in it clink. "Now you've heard the sound of my money. That should compensate you for my touching your bridge," she said, turning to leave.

Without warning, the bridge lord jumped up, aiming his feet for the tops of Miu Miu's feet. At the same time, he gave Miu Miu's chest a forceful push that could come only from someone trained in kung fu. Without her training, Miu Miu would have been uprooted like a rotten tree and dashed her head against the hard ground. The pint-size dwarf, her first roadblock, had caught her off guard.

But Miu Miu had detected a certain whisper of the ground beneath his feet, a certain ugly contortion of his bulbous body, his bones shifting, his shoulders slanting down, then up, to take flight, lifting off the ground. All this prejump split-second motion had seeped into Miu Miu's consciousness, igniting like fire.

Forewarned in that slow-motioned second, she turned her toes out fanlike, with heels riveted in place, so that the bridge lord would stomp down hard on the bare ground and not her toes as he intended.

But the dwarf sensed her shift. Staying airborne, he leaned forward with his stumpy arms pushed out, and his fingers curled into a Tiger's Claw position, ready to dig into Miu Miu's chest. Miu Miu countered with a Thunder Clap, slapping her palms together. Had she captured his hands, as she had intended, she would have crushed his fingers, rendering the lord powerless to count his ill-gotten coins. But the dwarf had already retrieved his thrusting arms and pulled his body into Leaning Pagoda, rerouting his *qi* and propelling him upward.

What a masterly reversal! Had she been blinded by pride or exhaustion, or was he from an exalted school of self-defense, capable of concealing his craft?

Even as she marveled, the little man effected an airy tumble away from Miu Miu and landed a deafening kick at her left ear with the blade of his foot. Miu Miu clutched her throbbing temple and collapsed to the ground.

Numbness spread from her temple down to her neck, stiffening it, and continued down to her chest. Could his fighting boots have been doused in poison? The numbness spread further south, crawling like centipedes into her lower belly. Her hips froze and her legs locked, but her mind never dimmed. She saw the short lord dust off his gown and give orders before leaving. A half dozen underlings suddenly surrounded her. Two men bent over her, ripped off the money pouch fastened around her waist, and took the dagger hidden in her boot. The taller one murmured something about rolling her over but paused as he lifted her robe and discovered Mother's rice cakes in the inside pocket. They took them, rolled her down to the water's edge, and hungrily stuffed the food into their mouths as they walked away.

Splash! Miu Miu fell into the water with Father's sword still intact, secured at her back. She couldn't move a toe. She was going to sink and drown!

She sank three times but slowly floated

back up each time, and was able to gasp mouthfuls of air through her frozen, parted lips. She stayed calm, still, and buoyant. She floated among tall lotus stems, propped up by the air that filled the dozen pockets hidden in Father's robe. Slowly she drifted away from Number One, passed beneath the span of Number Two and then Number Three and Number Four. She ceased counting after the fifteenth bridge, where she glimpsed the mighty Lord of Bridges again, beating up another traveler.

Before long the current picked up and the scenery blurred along the river banks. As the day surrendered its final glow, Miu Miu found herself floating among the city's other unwanted rubbish—a broken bamboo basket, some cracked gourd-shaped jars, and a floating corpse. Then in a sudden rush as the river narrowed and curved, she was washed onto the grassy shore of an empty inlet.

It was not until midnight that Miu Miu began to feel her body thaw from its frozen immobility. Searching around for a spot to rest for the night, Miu Miu climbed up the slope of the riverbank and found herself in a graveyard, surrounded by tombstones. All the graves seemed new, the soil still dark and fresh, bare of weeds. Some of the graves were still planted with incense sticks. Had there been an epidemic or a famine?

Death evidences itself whenever there is life. Master Wan's words exactly. But such memory soothed her not at all. Hungry ghosts remained hungry, ghosts though they might now be. She feared the coming of ghosts. She feared being mistaken for one of them. Searching and stumbling around the uneven ground fatigued her. Leaning against the tallest tombstone, she untied Father's sword from her back and hugged it to herself for protection against the wandering dead.

She recounted the day's wonders to keep herself alert. What had frozen her and then thawed her? How had she managed to float beneath more than fifty bridges unharmed and unhindered, to wash up safely on the only gentle patch of shoreline along the river? A sudden joy filled her at still being alive. No ghosts rose from their coffined sleep. Only early crickets sang while lanky grasshoppers leaped all around her. At the faint first crow of a rising rooster, she finally relaxed her guard and fell into deep, deathlike sleep.

Five 劍

THE BIG POST ROAD meandered among tall pines and thorny cactuses that bore meager flowers and pointy gray thorns as it entered Liao Dong Plateau, a rise in the warm central China plain where the temperature dropped to as much as thirty degrees cooler in the higher altitude. There was a flat road that wound around the vast base of the plateau; however, only a fool would go that way. Not only was it twice as long as the road that crossed the plateau, but thieves and bandits abounded there.

Miu Miu swallowed dryly as she looked up ahead. She had to reach Chang'an before the summer solstice—a day of festivities when the emperor would appear in public. The thought of all those sticky rice holiday treats wrapped in bamboo leaves, seasoned with minced pork and salted egg yolk fillings, made Miu Miu's mouth water and her throat itch. It was her fourth day away from home.

Night came and the road turned icy, too cold to continue. A low moon hung over the ridge, and the night quiet was sporadically disturbed by the hooting of owls and the howling of faraway wolves. Miu Miu slept in a cave, shivering until sunrise, and was awakened by a pack of shaggy mountain dogs. They poked and scratched the cave's mouth with their paws, searching for things to eat, driven away only when wild boars drove them downhill.

By first light, Miu Miu was on her way again as the warming sun crept up slowly and stealthily, thawing the crust of thin ice and melting frozen pearls of morning dew. At the top of the ridge sat a fortress. As she neared the looming structure, her eyes were drawn to a large, smooth rock, chiseled in red with the following words:

ALL TRAVELERS WILL BE SEARCHED.
NO SWORDS, ARROWS, OR KNIVES
ALLOWED BEYOND THIS POINT.
VIOLATORS WILL BE BEHEADED.
BY PERMANENT ORDER OF THE EMPEROR.

Travelers surrendered their weapons to the guards as they slowly passed one by one through a narrow passageway carved out under the fortress. Many were roughly patted down and searched.

Miu Miu could see her own breath form in the cold air as her teeth chattered nervously. Where was she going to hide the sword? What was she going to tell them if they asked the reason for her journey? She squatted down to grab a handful of snow and rubbed her face; the shocking chill refreshing her.

A caravan of a dozen carts and wagons wheeled past her, drawn by hairy water buffalos, brown and bulky, transporting crude moving hatcheries of live chickens and young chicks. All the hatcheries' split-bamboo roofs were covered by soft buffalo hides to keep the cold out. The chirping of chicks could be heard from inside, mixing with the squealing of axles and the groaning of wagon wheels. The big buffalos pulled their loads along with unblinking eyes and steaming breath, not needing the guidance of their dozing drivers.

Walking beside the noisiest carriage in the middle of the procession, Miu Miu swung up the side and crawled on top of a hatchery roof, hiding herself under the generous buffalo skin. No one seemed to have noticed her. Through the cracks in the roof, she could see all the young chicks inside, covered in yellow down, swaying with the cradlelike rhythm of the rolling cart. The sight made her homesick.

The caravan progressed slowly to a halt at the gate, whereupon Miu Miu could hear the cursing and abrupt questioning of one of the fortress guards. "What have got you in there?"

"Chicks, sir," a yawning rider near the front answered. "We are chicken farmers, poor and tired, making a meager living, traveling from town to town."

"A moving hatchery," the guard sneered. "Are you paying taxes to anyone?"

"Sure, sure, sir. The emperor is from Heaven and tax is his benevolence," the rider said, reiterating a common street chant. "Here is the proof of my payment." Miu Miu heard the rustling sound of paper. In a chaotic empire, crooked and corrupt, taxes were always collected on time and strictly recorded with seals and receipts. Even Mother's embroidery work and Miu Miu's own wood-gathering enterprise were subject to levies, and the receipts had to be kept readily on hand for any surprise inspections by tax officers.

One by one the guards searched the wagons, disturbing the chicks with sword tips shoved through the windows of the hatcheries, cracking unhatched eggs and frightening the hens. A guard stuck his head and arm inside the hatchery where Miu Miu was hiding. After stirring up the chicks violently, he stopped and stared up suspiciously at the roof, making Miu Miu shut her eyes and hold her breath.

"Your roof is hanging low. What do you have up there?" he demanded, poking his sword up through the thin roof, just missing her left leg.

The owner peered into the hatchery and said, puzzled, "It must be the leaks from last night's rain making the roof sag."

"It didn't rain last night on the plateau," the guard snarled, and sliced the blade of his sword along the feeble roof. It gave, caving in, and Miu Miu fell on top of the mother hens and their chicks. They went wild, flying into the guard's face.

"Rebel!" the guard shouted, his cry muffled by the chicken feathers in his mouth.

Miu Miu wasted no time. She leaped out of the cage and somersaulted over the two wagons in front of her. Then, running full out, she reached the other end of the passageway just as the guard dislodged his head from the hatchery window and shouted again, piercingly loud. Arrows flew past her head, and the gate began to descend. She just barely made it. The gate dropped shut with a heavy clang inches behind her, stopping the other guards from following her.

As the soldiers shouted for the gate to be raised back up, Miu Miu dashed forward like a ghostly shadow, zigzagging in an unpredictable pattern as more arrows shot her way. She dove off the path and flew off the edge of a steep cliff to land below on a rocky outcropping. From there she made her way silently downhill.

Before long, the guards' shouts grew faint and the fortress was forgotten. Her breath calmed. She was safe again, but for how long?

Six

ON THE SIXTH day, penniless and hungry, Miu Miu arrived on the outskirts of Chang'an. It was a mighty sight she saw, even from afar. The city walls loomed tall, and the palace cast long shadows. Chang'an sat like a mountain blocking the eastern horizon, and the golden roofs of the city's palatial mansions shone brilliantly in the morning sun.

Miu Miu was exhausted from her journey. Only once had she slept under a roof: in a stinking pigsty one rainy night, sharing her dreams with little piglets. The rest of the time she had lived in trees, abandoned temples, and rice-straw stacks along the fields and river-banks. She missed the little rice cakes that Mother had prepared for her, stolen from her by the Bridge Town bandits. All she had eaten was raw taro she had dug up from the earth and the thorny, red fruit she had picked from the smooth-barked lychee trees. When thirsty, she gulped water from deep wells or scooped it up from shallow ponds. The farther she journeyed away from Mother, the more she missed her rice cakes. She had picked the corners of her inside pockets and licked up each hidden crumb, remembering her mother cooking the rice and kneading the cakes together on her little stove. At that memory, Miu Miu had to blink away tears and bite her lips to keep back her sobs.

Her lips were parched and her eyebrows full of dust. Her hair was matted and shaggy, and Father's robe was wrinkled and torn. But as she stood by a clear pond, gazing at her own reflection, a smile crept to her lips. She looked manly, like a road-weary artisan or an itinerant warrior—the kind who were known to wander the rivers and traverse the forests, seeking the essence of kung fu, the purity of the greatest of all the martial arts.

Miu Miu cupped her hands and scooped a mouthful of spring water, disturbing the morning calm and frightening a pair of little frogs. One leaped frantically away into the grass; the other jumped into her hand. Gently, she returned it to the pond. It swam away, leaving behind a tiny fanning wake that rocked a fallen willow leaf like a boat.

The gate into the inner city surrounding the royal palace was guarded by men with heavy armor and tall steel helmets. Long *qiang*—spears—were in their hands, and short daggers were plunged into the sides of their boots. Some rode on horseback, tall as a wall; others traveled on foot, their boots clanking along the stone roadway. Still others paced the battlements atop the city walls while their comrades peered, ever vigilant, through arrow slits in the wall, ready for any sign of alarm.

Miu Miu did not enter through the gate right away. Judging from what she had observed, she would be stopped and sent back out the entrance, or worse, arrested for her dusty appearance and the sword in her possession. She strolled amid the morning throng, reading numerous official red posters splashed with black ink hanging on the walls. They were all arrest warrants, signed by the emperor, for rebels and agitators still at large.

In the glaring sun, under the arch of the imposing city gate, Miu Miu looked up and saw two hanging cages. Encased in each was a severed human head—two notorious rebels, Ar Piu and Ar Tong, known for roaming the part of the country near Miu Miu's village. Miu Miu had even run into one of them one morning, journeying to Goose Mountain.

She had encountered Ar Piu on a narrow path, a tall man on a thin mule, his feet nearly dragging the ground. He'd been trailed by a battalion of his men, dressed in green, with shaven heads. He had greeted her with a wave of his left arm—the right one was wrapped in a sling. She had heard that they had rampaged through some towns near Goose Village, taking the corrupt local magistrate's property and distributing all the land and loot to the poor villagers. They were heroes to her. But now Ar Piu's bloody head hung high from the city wall for thousands to see, and his eyes were dull like those of a dead fish. She wondered where his wounded right arm was and where his left one rested, the one that had waved to her.

As she took a last glance at his severed head, a vision of Father suddenly came to her. It was as if he were there in the cage and not Ar Piu: Father's head streaked with dried blood, and not the rebel's. It must be the morning sun playing tricks on her.

She closed her eyes, driving away the image of her father's face. It had no discernable features, for she had never seen his portrait. In her mind, Father's face was that of a kind man, smiling, with big eyes and a straight nose. The smiling face faded away, leaving a knot of sadness in her throat.

"What business do you have staring at the royal gate? What township do you come from?" a deep voice barked out. Miu Miu seemed to have caught a royal patrol guard's attention. She heard his shout, and from the corner of her eye she saw him strolling toward her. He wore ornate armor, with layers of feathery ornaments on his shoulders and hat, marking his elevated rank as an officer. Did he spot her because of her *qi*, her inner power? The *qi* plume could be seen only by eyes trained in the way of martial artistry of the highest order. The genuine masters were those who could not only sense their own *qi* but also see that of others, and not just its shape but its hue also, which indicated a person's intentions. A warrior who could see *qi* could prudently keep off his rival's path and pounce later.

Miu Miu had trained daily, but her artistry, advanced though it might be, hardly reached this degree of perfection. At her stage, some-where along the vast middling stretch where multitudes of other warriors nestled, the *qi* was fueled by tedious, feet-stomping training every day and hand-bleeding practice every night when she snuck out of bed to gain the power of the waning moon.

Master Wan had long warned her that learning was dangerous and artistry fateful. When she could be detected by those truly learnèd and did not yet have the ability to per-ceive them in turn, she would have entered the realm of danger. The monk had forbidden her from showing any of her tactics even in the simplest display to the meekest of the villagers. For such a manifestation would endanger not only herself and her mother but her master too. Thus she had remained the village wood girl, lugging her haul of the day off the tall moun-tain ridges and down the narrow path around the waist of hills, though she could have lifted five times the load on her single shoulder or carried as much with one arm, and run three times the speed and tenfold the distance. She had pledged to such meekness and had been truthful to it ever since without fault, except for now when she must have given off a tall plume of *qi,* her aura, in the color of burning red. That must be what had drawn the guard to her.

Hastily Miu Miu fell in step with the morning crowd, composed of vegetable merchants carrying dewy bok choi in round baskets, goose farmers with caged quackers swinging in the wind, fishermen with their stringed catch of the prior night strung over their wet shoulders, and flower girls with their blooms and blossoms bundled in leaky buckets crooked over their elbows.

The royal patrol guard tailed several yards behind Miu Miu, causing her to hasten and duck her head down, hiding among the geese, fish, twigs, and leaves of flowers, and wish herself small and negligible.

The gate was only yards away now. She would have to enter and perhaps be subject to the search randomly conducted by the diligent guards. Behind her, the shadowy patrol guard was closing in. She had been here less than the time it takes to boil water for tea, and already trouble was brewing.

Miu Miu looked frantically around her. A dozen breakfast tents were thronged with noodle-slurping, dough-chewing, *dou jian* drinkers sitting on stools, squatting on the ground, standing shoulder-to-shoulder, or leaning back-to-back. Miu Miu slipped her way among them, perching on a stool next to a young woman who was nursing her plump child, and pretended to be her companion. The woman threw a fit, squawking "Pervert!" and swinging her free hand at Miu Miu. The hungry baby, sensing the disturbance, pursed his mouth and let out an even fiercer scream, as if heaven had caved in. Miu Miu apologized profusely, nearly confessing her disguise. The woman's husband threw his hot *dou jian* at Miu Miu, wetting her robe, and chased her away.

Ducking lower, she made her way toward a squatting crowd of laborers with sweaty bodies and dusty faces made hot by the tofu soup they were slurping and the stinging sun shining down on them. They looked up at her with cold eyes.

"Dusty road," Miu Miu said apologetically, hoping that they would chat with her. The leader spat out his fried dough with a deep frown and cursed at her. "Stranger, go take a swim in the moat! You could kill a rat with your stench."

"I will if you will, too," Miu Miu said, hoping that such a provocation would bait the man into an expedient acquaintance.

The leader's frown deepened. "Are you challenging me, you lowly villager?" His face would have been handsome had it not been screwed into a knob of indignation.

She bit her lip, nodding. "You got the balls for it?" she asked boldly, as all Goose Village men would have done under such a circumstance.

Standing up, the leader reached out one hand and hooked his middle finger. "Let's hook on it."

After this there would be no turning back, no matter the peril or predicament, or honor would be forfeited.

Miu Miu extended her right hand to meet his, while glancing back at the royal patrol guard over her shoulder. He was still there, searching for her. She wondered if challenging this man would expose or camouflage her. She could bow out and vanish into the thickening crowd, but what would these men think of her if she raised a challenge only to forfeit it when the challenge was returned? It was just not done in her village. Goose Village might be small, but its honor loomed large, as solid as a rugged mountain. It had to be the same way in the village of this hot-blooded young man.

She hooked her middle finger through his, and they shook for a good three seconds. But when they were done, the young man would not let go of her. "Delicate fingers," he said thoughtfully.

"Yeah, like a girl's hand," another observed.

The leader shook her hand some more, nearly breaking her finger, but Miu Miu did not scream or beg to be let go. She kept her stare firmly fixed on his contorted face, the same way she had stared into the piercing eyes of a hungry wolf she had once encountered on a narrow mountain path, as she had been taught by her master. *Let your eyes be the daggers of strength, your body as still as a frozen tree.* Beasts would retreat from the power of such a stare, Master Wan had told her, and a well-trained opponent could topple his mightier foe, stabbed by such eyes.

The villager shook off her hand and spat into her face, landing a glob of saliva on her forehead, which dripped down to trickle over the bridge of her nose. "You are a girl, aren't you?" he accused, his sharp eyes darting up and down Miu Miu's body.

"She's worth a hundred taels of silver as a bride," muttered a boy on the right.

His companions shook their heads, disagreeing. "The stranger isn't a girl!"

"Let me be the judge of that," offered another with a hairy chest. Stuffing the rest of his fried dough into his mouth, he stood up and reached out his big hand for Miu Miu. "Let's see if you've got a turtle as big as ours hanging between your legs."

Miu Miu dropped her right hand with her five fingers spread wide in a move known as Opening the Fan, and blocked the young man neatly. She followed it with the complimentary move, Closing the Fan: clutching the young man's fingers and folding them backward. A hand wishing to fetch a turtle that was not there became a hand caught. The young man's knuckles cracked and his wrist bent backward, forcing him to kneel on the muddy ground, begging, "Let go, warrior of the road, please!"

"Who asked you to touch his turtle?" the leader asked.

"You wanted to know if he was a girl."

"Let go of him please, stranger," the leader said on his companion's behalf. "Du Du is a good fellow, though sometimes foolish as a duck."

Slowly Miu Miu reopened her fan, and Du Du, the hairy beast, crawled away.

"Fine. A warrior you are," the leader declared. "I shall take your challenge."

"A swim meet in the moat?" Miu Miu asked.

"No, a contest of fists in the forest." He pointed to the east. "Make way, fellows. You can go to the market and leave me alone to win this match."

"Why can't we come and watch?" Du Du asked, his face brightening.

"We are not performing jesters," the tall leader said.

"But who will carry you back if you lose?" asked Du Du.

The young man scowled. "Have you ever seen me lose?"

His three companions shook their heads.

"You should be afraid, stranger," her opponent warned.

Miu Miu just smiled.

The man jumped over a cage full of quacking ducks and Miu Miu followed him, but the hem of her baggy trousers caught on the cage's bamboo door, nearly pulling off her pants. As the cage door gave way, all the ducks fluttered out, scattering over peach stands, leek buckets, eel barrels, and wine pails, causing the farmers to chase after them, stirring up dust, which shielded them from the guard.

Quick-footed and light as the wind, the young man led Miu Miu to a forest of pines. Gnarled branches hung thick and low, and knobby trunks were rotted with ant-filled cavities. Roots crawled above the ground like earthworms, frozen in poses of futile escape, and thick tree beards swung darkly. The air was dense and the sun was blocked by the thick canopy of leaves. They came to a wide clearing shaded by pines, surely a stage of many prior martial-arts matches and challenges.

Standing ten feet away from her opponent, Miu Miu lowered her head in the obligatory salutation. *"Guo lu ren shuan bai."* Please let this traveler offer you his respect.

"Your respect I accept, but none in return is forthcoming." Instead of returning the bow, her opponent leaped up and punched Miu Miu right in her *duntien*, her lower abdomen, the source of her *qi*.

What a rude, sneaky blow. Such arrogance! Standing firm, Miu Miu countered with a tactic known as Muddy Crabhole, sucking in her *duntien* while filling up her chest with a lungful of *qi*. The maneuver caused Miu Miu's stomach muscles to wrap around his fist like the tentacles of an octopus. He twisted his fist to loosen the suction and tried to pull it back, but nothing gave. Changing his tactic, he drew a *qi* breath of his own. The power charge greatly expanding his chest, he channeled the flow sideways into his right arm, which was caught by her stomach muscles. A cold smile curled his lips.

He's concocting the Spinning Umbrella, Miu Miu warned herself. Such a move would either break his own wrist or spin and throw her far away, resulting in a smashed head or twisted neck. No one would be a winner in a contest between Muddy Crabhole versus Spinning Umbrella.

It's only the first pairing of tactics, Miu Miu thought, *and the match has already turned deadly.* She altered her flow of *qi* to blossom her tightly wrapped *duntien,* loosening her belly muscles so as to eject his fist out and away. "Aiiee!" She let out a shout of anger, trying to thrust the fist back, but his wrist seemed stuck to her belly button. Her muscles tautened rather than loosened, manipulated by the intrusion of his *qi* irrigating her innards as his fingers stretched wide like a fan to grab her spine so that he could hoist her up in the air and spin her like a parasol.

Let your tactic thaw and chaos will follow, Miu Miu heard Master Wan's voice say in her mind. *Deepen your faith and peace shall reign.*

She flattened her *duntien* farther inward, deepening the crabhole by tapping into the deep recesses of his *qi* flow and borrowing his power to strengthen her own. His cold smile vanished as his fist slackened in weakness, allowing her to grind his knuckles and wrist into temporary submission.

"Ah! You are cracking my hand!" the young man said between clenched teeth.

"And twisting your wrist!" Miu Miu cried triumphantly.

That little conceit was her first mistake.

That little seam in time and tactic was all the young man needed. He rose off his feet and started to spin himself in the direction of her twisting belly, leveraging his body weight, using his stuck right arm like an axle.

Miu Miu didn't yield. She spun herself like a windmill in full swing in the opposite direction. After several dizzying spins, both were screaming in pain. Another spin and his arm would be twisted beyond repair or her stomach muscles ripped off, depending upon whose might prevailed. They both decided to let go of their entanglement, at least for now, and flew thirty feet apart from each other. Miu Miu landed on a long branch. He arrived rather painfully on the fork of a pine tree, slamming his head back against the trunk. Hanging from the branch, Miu Miu gauged her foe and his next move while the young man did his best to dislodge himself. No sooner had he done so than he frog-leaped into the air, aimed straight at her. She swung sharply to meet him.

The man was soaring headfirst toward her, but Miu Miu was never a headlong leaper, given other choices. She spun her legs in the manner of a twirling *you tiao*, two strands of fried dough twisted together. The yarn of her *qi* lengthened out between them, aiming to catch the hotheaded one and toss him into the pond nearby to cool him off. But he cut her *qi* with a dagger of his own force and crashed into her. Her feet locked onto his shoulders and spun his whole body, tumbling him for several loops before landing him with a thud on the ground, his face buried in mud. He was quiet, huddling into the earth. Miu Miu wondered if he was preparing for a Snapping Turtle, a move that would sweep her off her feet and snap her hands off. But he remained still.

She dropped to the ground near him, ready for the ritual of *ren shu*, the concession of defeat. As she bent down to feel his pulse, her eyes caught sight of something that froze her. Thrown out of his shirt, a jade necklace dangled from his neck, exactly like the one belonging to her. She squatted down to glimpse the engraving on its face. That was mistake number two.

The man spat a breath of black *qi* her way, like a puff of dark smoke. Raising his head like a cobra, he sprayed his saliva all over her. It tasted bitter, like venom. He must have studied the eerie art of Qing Hai Mountain, whose followers infused their *qi* with a dead serpent's soul. The saliva instantly stung her eyes, pained her ears, and filled her nose with a bitter stench. In that blink of confusion, he leaped on her, pinning her down.

"Your necklace," Miu Miu gasped, writhing in agony. Under any other circumstances, it would have been a toss and flip, and she would have been on top. But she stayed pinned beneath him, though with one knee poking in his *duntien*, urgently straining to see what was written on the necklace dangling before her eyes.

"It's no one's business," he said, annoyed. "Tell me who you really are! Are you a royal scout for the emperor? Are you trying to get to my father through me?"

"No! I am no royal scout or provincial agent. Who is your father?"

"Ugly villager! One spit of venom hardly enough for you? Are you asking for another spray to blind you? Tell me who you are!"

"Just a wandering warrior. I only came to your breakfast tent to get away from a royal gate guard who was trailing me." She forced open her burning eyes wider and caught sight of the two characters engraved on the necklace as it spun at a new angle.

Miu Miu. Her name!

She dug in her hardened toes and kicked him off her, flipping him over to ride on his spine like a mule, with his face eating dirt again.

"What is your style of fighting?" the young man mumbled, his words muffled by weeds.

"Tell me who you are!"

"I am no one you should fear," he said, spitting out blades of grass. "We could be friends or foes. Your choice. I'm not afraid to die."

Miu Miu sank her hips down, squeezing a painful cry out of him.

"Why does your necklace have the name Miu Miu engraved on it?" she demanded.

"I am sworn to secrecy on that."

She ground her hips down once more, and he gave another yelp of pain.

"Miu Miu is the name of my bride-to-be," he said sullenly.

"Where is your bride-to-be?"

"You *are* a spiteful royal scout, aren't you?"

"No, I am not."

"I cannot tell you anything about Miu Miu. I'd rather die."

"I've heard that one before. To die is not brave. Once again, where is this bride of yours?"

"I don't know," he muttered, teeth clenched. "I haven't met her. I can tell you nothing else. What is your name, warrior?"

"Tell me yours first."

He hesitated. "Tong Ting of—"

"Cicada Village." Miu Miu's body softened as she slid off his back.

"How did you know my village?" he demanded, rolling to face her.

"Because I am Miu Miu."

"Of Goose Village?" The young man sat up, frowning, shock and disbelief filling his eyes. "Prove it," he said.

Reaching inside the collar of her robe, she brought out the necklace that had been safely bound and wrapped between her breasts.

"Almighty Buddha, a matching necklace!" Tong Ting looked up from the snake-style calligraphy engraving, greatly puzzled. "With my name on it? How did you come to possess this treasure?"

Miu Miu took off her hat and slowly unbound her long hair until it fell loose, pouring down over her shoulders.

Tong Ting reached out and clutched her hands, his eyes eager and bright. "Is it really you, Miu Miu of the south, seven days' journey by foot, who lives by the mountain with tall trees and the river full of geese?"

"It is I."

"Such small hands," he marveled.

Miu Miu's cheeks blushed like ripe autumn peaches. Ever since Mother had told her of the engagement, there had been this specter of a boy haunting her. She feared he might be short or stout, with yellow mouse teeth and sour breath. But here was this man before her, the husband who would never sire her offspring or warm her pillow or farm their fields and bring home sacks of pillowy rice. He was handsome, yes, yet he was to be only a footnote to her destiny.

"Tong Ting of Cicada Village . . . I can hardly believe it," she said, her heart racing. "It is our fate that we are linked for life, and it is our destiny that we meet in this manner. All Mother ever told me was the name of this shadow of a boy that I am linked to. Fate has us now in its fist. It is you who must tell me how we came to be matched and our fates intertwined."

Pressing Miu Miu's shoulders, he urged her to sit with him against a pine tree. Holding her hands, his eyes burning, he told her. "Your father was a legend. The man who paid with his life for his unparalleled skill in the making of swords. My father was his only apprentice, who learned the trade through years of building your father's fire, fanning his stove, pumping the bellows, brewing his tea, and emptying his chamberpot.

"My father asked your father once, as

apprentice to master, why he did not let his apprentice touch the hammer for the first five years of his apprenticeship. Your father said that it was because the essence of swordmaking lay in the art of fire making: how the iron is melted, the process through which a mere chunk of metal is transformed into a shining blade. Melting was the vital step, not hammering, not shaping, but the proper degree of heat, the correct rise of flames, the suitable timeliness of cooling. When all elements merged together according to the master's will and wish, the art is finessed, and steel fruit is born."

As he recounted the tale, Tong Ting held Miu Miu's hand tight. Occasionally Miu Miu pressed back, to encourage the flow of his words.

"When your father was murdered by the tyrant, my father and all the swordsmiths of this land mourned him. Some, like my father, stopped making swords and left the trade altogether. He didn't have much choice. They would have hunted him down had he remained in the trade. Father had to change his name, find a new trade, and move to another village, or the royal soldiers would have cut off his head as they did with all the rebels. It's rumored that there is a tribe of rebels and out-laws who carry black flags shaped like a sword, gathering and growing strength near the Tai Hu marshlands by the sea. They are said to be your father's followers, known as the Pure Blades."

"Father's followers? Are you one of them?"

"No, though how I wish I could be! But I could never find them."

"You still haven't told me why we were matched."

"Though your father and mine were master and apprentice, they were the closest of friends. It is customary in the trade that those who share the secret of swordmaking, that rare technique unknown to others, should keep such secrets among themselves by pledging their children to be wedded to one another. Though made blindly, such a pledge as ours seemed blessed. That is how we came to be matched. Tell me, Miu Miu, my betrothed, are you here to seek your groom? Tell me so, and we will return to the village temple and let the moon god be our arbiter of love as we are wedded, and a swordmaker of the next generation will soon be born to us," he said dreamily.

"Tong Ting, I am not here to find my groom or to seek matrimony." Her tone was somber, her voice firm. "I am here to fulfill that covenant defined under the terms of our betrothal."

"The terms of revenge."

"You know about it."

Tong Ting nodded, then covered his face with his hands. "I am ashamed that I am not the one to speak of revenge for your father, my own father's master. I am humiliated that it is you who had the steely backbone to speak of it." He slapped his face with his rough hands until Miu Miu grabbed them in hers.

"Stop that!" Miu Miu cried. "There is no need for shame. The terms have changed. I alone will carry out this covenant."

"No, this covenant must be carried out by both of us," Tong Ting said. Twisting out of her grip, he held her hands tenderly. "You cannot deprive me of this right. It is also my birthright. We will cleanse both our fathers' names together, and take back the honor of our fathers' fellowship."

"Very well, together," she said softly. Pulling back from him, Miu Miu untied the sheath from her back and pulled out the treasure.

"The female sword!" Tong Ting uttered in sheer excitement. "May I hold it?"

Pleased that he knew of her sword, Miu Miu handed it over. He gripped the handle with a firm hand, waving the long and elegant blade so that it caught the sun. A dazzling array of reflections danced along the blade, scaring a few crows from the trees. "Do not show it off or others will detect its shine," Miu Miu cautioned.

"What a treasure! Just as Father told me,"

Tong Ting exclaimed, letting his middle finger glide along the blade. A stream of blood crawled down the sharp length. "Lick my blood," he murmured, "for such is my pledge of bravery and loyalty to you, my accomplice."

Her heart racing, utterly unprepared for such a show of gallantry, she lowered her head and parted her lips. Slowly, her tongue licked along the length of the blade, lapping up the blood from Tong Ting's finger. It tasted like metal, like yellow wine, like revenge. When she lifted her head up, her lips and the corners of her mouth were smeared with red. Gently, Tong Ting wiped the stains from her lips with his still bleeding hand.

Blood for blood, Miu Miu thought, rolling up her sleeves. Slowly and deliberately, she sliced the blade of her father's sword along her forearm. Big fat droplets of her blood tumbled down the roundness of her arm, falling in an urgent stream straight into Tong Ting's waiting mouth. Her blood gleamed in the sun like a long ruby chain as Tong Ting swallowed.

When he looked up, he had tears in his eyes.

"Why are you crying?" Miu Miu whispered.

"My tears are for us. Now we are wed. Blood to blood, flesh to flesh. You have fulfilled your father's pledge to be given to me. Now I have to fulfill mine: to avenge the father who bore you. If I am to die, then let death be my path."

"And mine too," she said. After a long lull, she added, "But we won't die, now that I have you watching my back, and you have me guarding your flanks."

"Our foe is formidable, our goal nearly impossible," he reminded her soberly. "There are a thousand guards patrolling the inner city, another one thousand guarding the royal palace. Emperor Ching himself is surrounded by a hundred of the fiercest warriors armed with deadly swords and the sharpest arrows. No one can come near him, and no ghosts dare hover over that seed of evil. Not even your father's sword can aid us far in our pursuit. We couldn't even enter the outer gate without being arrested." Pulling up a pant leg, he untied a strap fastened to the top of his boot, revealing a finely crafted dagger, unsheathed. Yanking off a few strands of hair from his head, he let them fall onto the blade. His dagger neatly sliced the falling hairs, one by one. "Father secretly made this for me. Deadly though it might be, I was afraid that it would never ever see the blood of its enemy. I've carried it ever since I turned twelve. It's the only weapon my father made after he changed his trade."

"When does Emperor Ching leaves his palace?" Miu Miu asked.

"This noon when the sun reaches the extreme arc of the heavens."

"This noon!" Miu Miu stood up, pulling Tong Ting up from where he still knelt.

"Yes. He will be traveling out of his palace through the inner city streets, heading to the platform facing the Temple of Heaven. There he will offer his annual prayer to his ancestors for a bumper harvest in the Summer Festival ceremony. He does not leave the palace again until winter solstice."

"It is our moment, then. We must go to the inner city now." Squinting, Miu Miu gazed up at the sun, which had already climbed midway along its morning ascent.

"How are we going to enter the city gate?" Tong Ting asked.

"You wait." Going behind the thick tree trunk, Miu Miu peeled off her outer robe and unwrapped, layer by layer, the long red silk sash she had fastened around her bosom to flatten her chest. When she had finished unraveling the tight loops of punishing silk, Miu Miu exhaled a long breath. Behind her, Miu Miu heard Tong Ting groan. Turning, she caught him peeking at her. "Get away. Don't look," she admonished, but his avid eyes stayed fastened on her.

"You have bruises. I know of an herb nearby whose juice will soothe those marks."

"Close your eyes. You are shaming me."

Tong Ting smiled, leaning against the tree,

his eyes drinking in her creamy skin, the tender small of her back. "If we are going to die today, why should we be ashamed of loving each other?"

Donning her inner robe once more, she made her way to the pond. Squatting, she splashed water against her skin. The coolness caused goose bumps to rise up on her back and chest. "Death does not end things on earth," she said.

"It doesn't?"

"No. We were matched even before we were born. We should be bound together after our earthly lives end."

"You sound like my father. He is a fortune-teller and ghost chaser nowadays," Tong Ting said.

"It's true. Ghosts do live on after death. I talk to my father's ghost every day in my mind. I feel him whispering into my ear as if he were talking to me, face-to-face." She combed her wet fingers through her long hair, sprinkling it with pearly drops of water, then neatly braided her hair into one thick rope before coiling it into a bun at the back of her head in the same way she had seen her mother do every morning at her mirror. Miu Miu had tried it in the secrecy of her own bedroom, imagining her wedding day, when her heart would be beating swiftly at the prospect of beginning life with a stranger. Today she felt no such shyness, nor the sweetness she usually felt in the pretense. Rather it was the coolness of reality, of destiny, that was slowly dawning upon her. When she turned, Tong Ting stared at her, his square jaw hanging agape.

"*Sha gua.*" Fool, she called him. "Let's get ready." All the men in the village had stared at Miu Miu that way, as they had sat sipping tea on the days she passed by Goose Bridge wearing a mountain wildflower in her hair.

"Where are you going to hide the sword?" Tong Ting asked, finally closing his mouth. "If they find it, we will lose our heads before anything is accomplished."

"Leave that to me." Spreading her robe on

the ground, Miu Miu carefully placed the sheathed sword on it, folding the sleeves in and tugging the hem up snug to form a little bundle. She ripped the red silk sash into two pieces, one of which she tied around her forehead. The other piece she draped over the sword.

"I understand," Tong Ting said, nodding. "The red headband marks you as one who has just given birth to an infant. The robe, with the sword bundled in it, becomes the newborn."

"And we are the panicking parents who must rush this dying baby to seek help from a good doctor who lives within the inner city," Miu Miu said with determination.

Tong Ting leaped to his feet, following in Miu Miu's wake.

Seven 劍

"YOU WALK TO the left of me," Miu Miu told Tong Ting, holding her "sick infant" tenderly in her arms, as they vied to gain a foothold among the thickening noon throng.

"No. Men all walk on the right side of their wives," Tong Ting said, nodding to some examples in the crowd.

"Those men are so careless of their wives, they care not which side they walk on. See, they are looking at the flower girls strolling by the side of the road."

"Why does it matter which side I walk on, as long as we enter the gate unchecked and safe?" Tong Ting asked stubbornly, striding along like other men, seemingly uninterested in the company they were keeping. He saw his fellow day laborers in the distance, with whom he had parted earlier, and waved to them.

Twenty yards away from the gate, Miu Miu spotted the royal patrol guard again, the same one who had followed her earlier. Her heart tightened into a knot. The man stood tall and vigilant, looking far and wide for any sign of trouble coming to the gate.

"Where are you going?" she whispered as Tong Ting disappeared from her sight, vanishing into the crowd. Just as quickly, he returned with flowers in his hand and a large green lotus leaf.

"Flowers for your hair, and a lotus leaf to block the sun from our sick baby," Tong Ting said, inserting two white lilies into Miu Miu's headband. He held the lotus leaf up to shade the infant bundle from the sun, like a concerned father who did not want a single ray of sunlight touching his precious offspring. Miu Miu, who had thought to stomp Tong Ting's foot to punish him, changed her mind at his thoughtfulness.

"Now lean over my shoulder, a bit closer," Tong Ting suggested. "Pretend you're very worried about the baby. He's a boy, isn't he?"

"Does he look like a boy?" Miu Miu snapped back in irritation.

"He has to be a boy."

"Why not a girl?" she argued.

"I want a boy," he insisted.

"It doesn't matter what you want. This is not about you."

"But it is about me. If it is not a boy, then I will not be as concerned because a girl is just someone we will raise to age fifteen and marry off to be some man's wife."

"Like me?"

"Er . . . yes, like you."

"So you don't think much of me?"

"I do. I do think much of you. To prove it, I will tell you this. I long had my eyes on a girl from Willow Village—where we moved to. My heart was beginning to throb for her. But Mother stung me with burning incense on my arm, and Father whacked a ladle against my head to remind me of the necklace that was given me, a pledge that, no matter the distance and all the things in between . . . "

Now Miu Miu was truly incensed. This boy should not talk at all, she concluded. All he did was spill dark poison that would make any girl sour with anger. What a foolish young man he was, boasting of his liking and straying. Yes, straying. Men weren't allowed to stray: They had to be like rock, firm and lasting, whereas women were like water, changeable and yielding.

She'd had her fancies too. Like the black-smith who had smiled at her whenever she passed by his shop. He would wait there with a grin on his face, his oily beads of sweat gliding down his muscled shoulders, his face dark and dirty but handsome. Or the sweet village scholar, poor but dignified and ambitious, who

111

wanted to pass the civil service exam held every six years and be plucked out of poverty by the royal palace to serve the sovereign. The scholar had written poems for her with water, for he could afford neither ink nor a silk scroll. Someday, the scholar told her, he would write his daily poem for her on satin from Suchow, with the smoothest and darkest ink from Lan Tien. Each poem would be more soulful and lyrical, more full of love and passion, than any yet known to man, and the girl who walked the mountain every day and sold her fuel every nightfall would be famous. Miu Miu had asked him why he had wanted her, a poor wood girl without a dowry. He had told her that she had a natural beauty like the sun unadorned, the moon unveiled, the river untamed: that was what the poor poet had said of her. And she had other admirers as well—the sesame-oil man, the cobbler, the local magistrate who had several concubines. All these men had shown their favor by giving her gifts during the Spring Festival and summer celebration.

At the same time, Miu Miu saw enough cruelty around her to wonder sometimes if perhaps she was better off alone with her mother. The women of the village were like plows with which men blindly tilled the land, or the sharp sickles with which they cut the ripened rice. In fact, some men took better care of their tools, shining and sharpening their sickle blades so they did not rust the next season, and tenderly cleaning the mud off their plows and repainting them. Some even gave pet names to their tools, but what did they call their wives? Not by their names, but by the *hey*s, *hah*s, and *you*s that came roughly out of their mouths.

The rich man down the street would every day at sunset ravish his third wife, a young girl of fifteen, until she screeched for help. Whenever the girl tried to refuse his attentions, he would beat her black and blue, then subject her to the same fate the next day. Even her parents, a timid couple who depended on their aging son-in-law for provisions, aided the devil by sending the lamb back into the tiger's mouth each time she sought refuge with them.

Images of those women made Miu Miu doubtful of her betrothal pledge.

"Why do you talk of this girl when you are with me?" Miu Miu demanded, scowling at Tong Ting.

"Well, that's her," he said, pointing to a flower girl walking a little way behind them. "She's the one who gave me the flowers and the lotus leaf."

"That flower girl?" Miu Miu looked her way, and saw that the girl's hair was long and braided, hanging tantalizingly down over her shapely, plump chest. Her eyes were dark, her lashes long and vivid, and her voice sweet like a nightingale, calling passersby's attention to her dewy blooms arranged like a rainbow in her buckets.

"Do you still fancy her?" Miu Miu demanded.

"Well . . ."

"Well what?"

"Well, she . . ."

In that small pause, Miu Miu felt a sourness of feeling rise up within her, plucking discordantly on her heartstrings, throbbing her temples, making the tips of her ears and her cheeks burn red. Was she feeling the devilish thing other women called "drinking vinegar" that made your stomach sour and heart bitter—what second, third, and fourth wives often talked about during their gossipy embroidery afternoons with her mother? All the rich men sent their young wives to Mother, not to learn embroidery as a trade but more as a leisurely hobby to occupy their time.

"Well . . . what?" Miu Miu demanded bitterly.

"Well, she said you're quite pretty."

Instead of feeling flattered, Miu Miu felt the slight sting of insult, as if the intimacy she shared with Tong Ting had been intruded upon by the unwanted praise of another. "Who asked her for her opinion?"

"I did," Tong Ting replied, looking rather pleased with himself.

"Why? Because you weren't sure of me?"

"But I was."

"Then why ask anyone, if you are sure? Why ask her? Is she your mother? Your auntie? Your grandmother?"

"Miu Miu," Tong Ting said, baffled, "why are you angry at me? She is my best friend."

"You haven't seen angry yet," Miu Miu fumed. "Now she is your best friend!" Lifting up her left foot, she stomped hard on Tong Ting's foot.

"*Ow!* What did you do that for?"

"How good a friend is she to you?" Miu Miu asked. "Did she rub your sore back?"

"No!" Clutching his foot, he stared at her like she was crazy.

"Did she embroider you a money pouch?"

"No, that is for lovers."

"Well, you talk like you are lovers. Did you love her?"

"No," Tong Ting said shortly, growing angry himself. "Why are you talking all this nonsense?"

"Why? Because we were born for each other, and now you fancy another even while you wear my necklace. Does she know about your betrothal necklace?"

"I am sorry I mentioned her," Tong Ting muttered, limping painfully behind her. "We are almost at the outer gate. Can we just drop the subject? You are the only one that I have fancied as my bride."

"I am?" She stopped and faced him.

"I swear by the name of Buddha," Tong Ting said earnestly.

"Why didn't you say so in the first place?"

"I have tasted your blood, and you mine. Isn't that enough?"

Satisfied, Miu Miu turned back toward the gate, hastening her steps to appear as if she were hurrying. People flowed toward the congested gate from all directions, like rivers reaching the final sea. The gate measured no less than twenty yards across and ten high. Guards were ranked thickly along the city wall, standing in close formation across the broad walkway like a fishing net spread to catch any roving rogues, rebels, and assassins and prevent them from coming through. Standing in a row, they stared closely at those entering, judging them as the gate guards below searched though their buckets and rummaged through their sacks of rice, bags of wheat, barrels of live fish, bundles of bok choi, and cages of monkeys. One guard loosened a man's robe and searched his inner pockets, while another unwrapped the quilt of an infant soundly asleep in a carrier cradled in his mother's arms.

"See, they are even checking the baby bundles," Tong Ting muttered.

"You pretend to grieve. Let me worry," Miu Miu muttered, darting her eyes around, making certain that the patrol guard who had sniffed her out somehow at the outset of the day wasn't tailing them or watching them from afar. She sensed that the vigilant patrol guard wasn't like the stationary guards who worked like roadblocks. This man was a floating agent walking a random beat. When suspicion or intuition warranted, he would pounce on the unsuspecting subjects and take them to be interrogated until they confessed to crimes—even those they'd had no intention of committing. He would torture them, and when released, they would crawl away, too fearful to ever tell their story.

But he was nowhere around. Probably chasing after another or still pursuing Miu Miu's lost shadow, a shaggy young man smelling of the road and vast country where discontent brewed and uprisings were rampant.

"What is your hurry?" demanded a glaring farmer. "You knocked my mother goose—hear how loud she's honking! Slow down. We all have to go through the checkpoint."

"Our child is dying," Tong Ting said. "Please make way."

"My carps are dying, too. If you keep on shoving my barrels the way you are doing, they'll die sooner," complained a fisherman, swinging his jostled barrels at Tong Ting. Tong

Ting and Miu Miu dodged the angry fisherman and squeezed closer toward the mouth of the city, where the line entering the gate became an orderly trickle. No one dared look at the gate guards, who stood clothed in steel armor and helmets with clinking neck plates. In their hands were long spears and fierce swords, some doubled-edged, others with hooked tips. Still others were armed with bows and arrows, their faces covered with steel masks, making their features appear flat, solemn, and death-like. Yet more guards were on horseback—riding Gobi stallions that flicked their thick tails, chasing away the summer flies buzzing around their massive buttocks.

No matter the urgency, the throng progressed at only a snail's pace, for each traveler was a threat to be reckoned with so that their sovereign, the emperor, could perpetuate his corrupt reign and let prosperity trickle down to his chosen soldiers, who passed down their inheritable legacy to their heirs.

At the checkpoint two guards greeted them

with their stern masks, their eyes hidden behind a pair of slits. Miu Miu rocked her baby as if to soothe it, murmuring a gibberish of love and worry that she imagined a mother sickened with desperation would utter. She had once seen a widow wailing at a funeral procession in Goose Village. It was unlike anything she had ever heard, something coming from the depths of the widow's soul, guttural and harsh. The bereaved woman had clung so hard to her husband's corpse—a drowned fisherman who had left behind seven little ones and two sets of aging elders—that she had to be pried away.

Miu Miu mimicked that widow now, choked sounds coming from her throat. She expanded her chest and let the sound pass out of her. The first cry shocked her, Tong Ting also, and those standing before and behind them. Garbled words and mangled syllables poured out of her. "My baby! My baby is dying. Let me pass so we can hurry the child to the doctor!" Overcome by her worry and grief, she collapsed sobbing in Tong Ting's arms.

"Unbundle the infant and tell us the name of the doctor you are to visit," the masked guard demanded. Miu Miu was certain that he was indeed a living human and not a statue only when she spotted hairy strands of the guard's mustache poking out from the mouth guard.

"My woman just gave birth to our first child ten days ago," Tong Ting said, waving his lotus leaf at the flies buzzing around Miu Miu and her bundle.

The royal guard took an involuntary step back. "Ten days ago! Didn't anyone tell you that she is still dirty with birth blood? She should have stayed hidden away out of the sun until the curse of birthing faded away." He covered his mouth with his free hand, bending an iron elbow, making a clanking, squeaky noise.

"Yes, we know of her curse and dirtiness, and that she is not to see the sun or be exposed to the northern wind, whose gale could enter her open pores and make her joints sore. But the baby is dying, and my wife has to breastfeed it. We have to rush the babe to the doctor."

"For what?"

"He has to cut the baby's belly open and take out the poisoning pus. They say that is the only hope for our child."

When the guard's hand reached out to unwrap the baby, Miu Miu let out another wail that swelled her throat like a young rooster crowing, making it bulge red, spraying saliva onto his hand.

"Why is she wailing like that?" the guard asked angrily, jerking his hand back.

"She has been poisoned. The baby suckling on her milk passed the poison to her, making her mad."

"Then you should not be allowed in. The entire city and palace will be poisoned," said another voice, deep and assured. Peeking through her tears, Miu Miu saw with dismay that it was the tall patrol guard who had shadowed her that morning. Both Miu Miu and

Tong Ting froze at his ominous statement.

"But the poison, our village doctor said, does not spread by touch or through the air," Tong Ting assured him. "It is only through the milk that it can run between mother and infant. See, I remain in good health."

The rest of the crowd had shrunk back from them ever since the word *poison* had been uttered. The officer, however, took two steps closer to them. "If your village doctor knew what it was and how to treat those afflicted, why seek help elsewhere?"

"The city doctor we seek inside these walls is the teacher of our humble village doctor."

"Is that so?" The officer cast his eyes over Miu Miu's form, bent down low over the bundle. Her shoulders shook and lips quivered as if she were overwhelmed by her grief. The officer turned his dead-oyster eyes back on Tong Ting and said, "You look familiar."

"I have passed through this gate many times to seek work."

"You are one of the day laborers who flow

in and out of the city like garbage, aren't you?" the officer asked, making Tong Ting fidget uneasily. "Where are your fellow laborers?"

"They have gone ahead, officer."

"Gate Commander Han," the man corrected him.

"Gate Commander Han. If I may say so, you have a good memory, seeing thousands come and go every day."

A cold smile curled the commander's lips. "Flattery will not get you an inch farther."

The damned commander was peeling Tong Ting layer by layer with sinister deliberation, Miu Miu thought with a sick feeling in the pit of her stomach. Another mishap and their enterprise would be in jeopardy. *"Aaiee!"* Miu Miu cried. Dropping onto the dusty ground with her infant beneath her, she proceeded to yell in a choking, sobbing, retching manner as her eyes rolled and saliva flew. Her free hand tore at her red silk headband, pulling her hair and crushing the flowers in it until her hair resembled a bird's nest.

"Shut her up while we conduct our affairs," the gate commander snapped. "That is, if you want your child seen by the city doctor by sunset."

Not knowing what else to do, Tong Ting slapped Miu Miu across her cheek. But she persisted in her madness, wailing and spitting, prompting Tong Ting to slap her again, hard enough to spin her head sideways and make her grit her teeth.

"You are a husband who knows when to be forceful," the commander said, praising him, as her wailing subsided into muffled sobs.

Miu Miu hated the officer, and she hated Tong Ting even more as he openly preened at the compliment.

"I can only let both of you enter through this gate if you can pass the following test for me. Take a few steps back away from her," the gate commander said.

"What test is this?" Tong Ting asked, stepping away from Miu Miu, unsure of what to do with the lotus leaf he still held.

Waving Tong Ting over to the desk by the gate where a bearded notary sat, the gate commander gave him a piece of rice paper and a writing brush. "Write down the name of your village and the sex of your new child. I shall ask your woman the same questions. Your answers had better match."

Tong Ting was stunned. They had talked of Cicada Village, where he originally was from, and Willow Village, where he had moved. Then there was Goose Village, where she lived. Which would Miu Miu choose? And more troubling was the second question. He had wanted the bundled sword to be a boy, and she a girl. Tong Ting scratched his head and frowned.

"But my wife doesn't write," Tong Ting said. "She knows no words, and as you see, is ravaged with madness."

"Worry about yourself. I will ask her the questions myself." Strolling over to Miu Miu, he whispered into her ears.

Gingerly, Tong Ting wrote down whatever

127

came to his mind first. Goose Village and a boy. Truth and wishful fancy. He prayed to the mighty Heaven and the good Buddha, whom he occasionally worshiped, and the earth god he prayed to daily for a good day's earning or a good night's catch.

Why Goose Village? Why a boy? He did not know. It just seemed right.

When the gate commander returned and read what Tong Ting had written, he smiled and said to Tong Ting, "Your wife is as mad as you say she is. Take her and clear the passageway for others."

Unable to believe his ears, Tong Ting hurried over to Miu Miu, who was sitting on the ground like a child, rocking back and forth, her eyes dazed, saliva dribbling down her chin. Helping her up, he rushed her quickly through the gate. They merged into the throng like a pair of small fish, losing themselves on the human tide that floated into the inner city.

Eight

"WHAT LUCK THAT we still have our necks," Tong Ting cried, his words bursting out in a harsh whisper as he urged Miu Miu along. The crowd dispersed into a web of small streets and hidden lanes that fanned off from the gate.

"Be careful—don't talk so loud. They are everywhere. See there, by the incense store." She gestured to the royal guards watching the people from their post in an elevated box at the corner of the street where they stood guard.

"Which sex did you say our baby was, and

what village did you name?" Tong Ting asked curiously.

"What did you write on your paper?" Miu Miu asked in return.

"I said a boy, and that we were from Goose Village. So what was your answer?"

"I told him none of that. I said that I was from a flock of villages, maybe Duck Village, Turtle Village, Cicada Village, or Willow Village. I finally settled on Cow Village. I told him my husband looked like a cow as other men of Bull Village do."

"And what gender did you say our child was?"

"A calf or a duckling or a seedling."

"We could have lost our necks!"

"But we didn't."

"How could you be so bold to make jest out of his questions?" Tong Ting wondered. "And how clever of you to play it up and profit from your madness!"

"No, you are the clever one. You gave me the cues to follow."

He put his arm around her shoulders, giving her a squeeze, and got a slap back in return.

"We are not clear of the danger yet," she warned, throwing off his arm.

"Our luck at the gate makes me feel as if we can fulfill any task together."

"Luck will run thin. Strategy is what we need. I am only a country girl. Tell me, city boy, where do we go from here? I am lost. You have been here before, haven't you?"

"Every day of my life since I turned twelve, I have been coming to this city, helping my father carry his fortune-teller stand, his ghost-chasing spade, and his heavy cloak."

"What does he do here?"

"Here in the city he is a funeral weeper," Tong Ting said. "Sometimes the son of a wealthy family is so happy about his father's death that tears are hard to come by. Father cries so well that he sometimes even moves those coldhearted rich sons to tears. He is almost never out of work. There is always death as there is life."

"What luck to be such a good weeper in a big city like this."

"It is no luck, really. He has red, teary eyes after years of manning the hot stove for your father, and he pretends that it is his own wife whom he is mourning, not some stranger. My mother died when I was a young boy," he said quietly, prompting Miu Miu to squeeze his arm in comfort.

The inner city looked like the stage of the regional operas performed in her muddy village square during the Spring Festival. From roof to roof, colorful banners were strung across the streets. Red lanterns hung from them with the characters for *longevity* and *harvest* painted on them in gold. The sounds of the bamboo flutes and the plucking of pipas mixed with the blaring of trumpets and the beating of snakeskin drums. Children set off firecrackers from their fathers' ground-floor storefronts, their grandfathers' tearooms, and their grandmothers' embroidery chambers screened off from the din of the street by silk drapery. The firecrackers

sounded like a bursting beehive, making pop-
ping sounds like the cracking of hollow bamboo poles. When the bursting died down, the
air was infused with the pungent smell of gun-
powder, reminding Miu Miu of early Spring
Festival mornings, when firecrackers were lit to
chase away evil creatures called *nien* and to
welcome the new year. But somehow the sound
of firecrackers didn't seem fitting on this warm
summer day, and the band music sounded to
Miu Miu full of lamentation and sadness, like
a dirge. Could this be the sound of her destiny?

She looked around with interest at this
walled-in enclave and saw herself like a charac-
ter in a drama staged on the streets of the inner
city, heading to her destined end, playing a part
written for her by fate. The music was played
not in anticipation of the emperor's holy
prayers but for her, an ordinary daughter of the
earth, coming to terms with an extraordinary
pledge. Her life would end here under this glaring noon sun, but only after the pledge was carried out. She was but a droplet in a raging river

that was her bloodline, slowly easing through the flat delta toward the sea. A droplet, no more and no less.

"We are near Tian Tang Square, where the emperor will pray," Tong Ting murmured as the street widened out. Before her stood a soaring pagoda with purple roofs rising up and up. Its uppermost golden dome glinted and gleamed under the sunlight, dazzling her.

Golden throne. Royal purple. The signs of the emperor's godly reign.

No commoner was allowed to wear the color purple in the presence of the sovereign. To do so would violate the will of Heaven, and the offender would be condemned to be flayed or have a limb cut off.

Miu Miu had met a woman once who'd had her arms and legs severed because her son, a rebel, had dared call himself the Purple Monarch, leading an army of two thousand peasants. They had been squashed like mosquitoes. What, then, she wondered, was the punishment for killing the emperor?

Miu Miu felt as if it were with her father's eyes that she scanned the scene around her, seeing the pious subjects of the sovereign bent down in a kneeling mass on the dusty square surrounding the pagoda with flowers in their hands, their faces turned down to the earth, as if the sight of the emperor would blind them. It was with her father's ears that she listened and heard the sounds of horses' hooves shaking the earth, making pebbles and particles of soil tremble as they neared—the royal entourage, coming with its troop of fawning eunuchs and haughty guards, forcing their way through the crowded thoroughfares and congested boulevards on their tall stallions.

Miu Miu's pulse quickened, each heartbeat making her temples thump like the high tide beating against the shore. She became light-headed for a moment, forced to lean on Tong Ting's arm, which made him ask with concern, "What's the matter? Is it the heat?"

"No, just Father's blood racing through my veins, his will making its demand, his thoughts giving me a plan."

"I too have a plan," Tong Ting whispered as they watched from the edge of the crowd gathered in the square, which was composed of sweaty country merchants who had interrupted their day's affairs to witness this display of royal grandeur. By attending the Heaven-thanking ceremony, they hoped to gain a blessing to make their stores more crowded with business, and their land grow more abundant harvests. There would always be typhoons that drowned their rice and floods that rotted their yams, droughts that dried their land and plague that killed their young. Thanking Heaven was their sole safeguard against the unpredictable future.

Among them were the inner-city folk: finely dressed ladies in sedan chairs, descending from their seats, their silk handkerchiefs waving away the sweaty merchants' stench and ped-dlers' smells. Miu Miu could smell the ladies' fragrant perfume and the thinner scent of their makeup powder. With them were their silk-clad, mustached city men—known for their winking and nose-rubbing habits, the result of their opium-puffing addiction—their robes' outer pockets sunken low with silver and gold coins. They were there not to accompany their wives or their concubines, but because the head of each household was expected to attend whenever the sovereign was expected within the city, regardless of the weather. For if they were not there, a visit from the emperor's agents would find those absent and inquire about the cause of such dereliction of duty. The agents would be made aware of such absences by the spying ears and eyes scattered within each neighborhood, reporting through secret channels, up and up, until their reports reached the very top of the hierarchy. Then one lowly officer would be sent to investigate that absentee, inquiring about his whereabouts and the cause for such a misdemeanor, so that his punishment could be meted out accordingly.

"Look at that pine tree," Tong Ting murmured, pointing with his thumb to the side of the square, interrupting Miu Miu's thoughts. The tree was tall and thick, with its limbs long and hanging beards untrimmed. One far-reaching branch in particular stretched nearly halfway to the square's center. "A perfect branch to leap onto when the time comes for the emperor to bow down to pray," Tong Ting whispered. "No one will be looking up. His men will be on their knees with their heads bent low to the earth. Even the most vigilant must obey that rule. I can jump up there without anyone seeing me."

"You?" She turned to gaze into his dark eyes. "I thought we settled this matter already."

"I will be shamed if I let you take the lead."

"Tong Ting, shame will never befall you," she whispered, moved by his valor. "You have already shown me the utmost bravery. But I must be the one to render the killing blow."

Pain creased his face. "And you are a finer warrior than I."

"You let me win our first bout."

"No, I didn't. But if we survive this day, would you grant me the honor of learning from you?"

Nodding, she leaned her head on his strong shoulder. "Thank you, Tong Ting. I don't feel alone in this pursuit anymore."

"You will never be alone again for as long as I live."

His simple words touched Miu Miu.

"If you are determined to do the deed yourself, this is what you must do," he whispered. "Be ready to leap up to the farthest tip of that long branch—"

"Using it to bounce off to the center of the square," Miu Miu finished.

"Look," Tong Ting said, as something caught his attention. "The gate commander is circling the north end of the square."

Miu Miu glanced in the direction Tong Ting indicated and saw the fluffy purple feathers of the commander's hat in the distance, hovering a foot above everyone else. "Is he looking for us?"

"He very well might be. We didn't exactly go and seek that doctor on Medicine Lane."

"We must be discreet then," Miu Miu said, hugging the bundled sword.

"Is your sword ready?" Tong Ting asked in a whisper.

"As ready as the day it was made by its master."

"Do you know where the sword should cut?"

"On the neck."

"No, not there. The emperor is known to wear a steel guard to protect the neck."

"Then his chest?"

"He wears armor under his silk gown too."

"His face?"

"He wears a steel mask."

"Where should I strike then?"

"His groin. It's the one area that can never be covered according to the will of Heaven. It's the source from which the sacred seed flows. It is never to be encumbered by anything and is left unguarded, no matter the risk or peril.

That's where the sword should go."

"How do you know so much about him?" Miu Miu asked.

"All my life I knew we would one day face him as we do today. I could have been a goose farmer, taking flocks to the river to chase after the floating worms, counting the eggs they lay every night, selling them in Willow Village square, and returning home by early afternoon to cook supper. Instead, I have been coming to the city as a day laborer to seek knowledge about the emperor. I could never gain such knowledge living in Willow Village." Nudging Miu Miu, he said, "Look, the gate commander is making his way deliberately toward us."

Miu Miu was struck by the single-mindedness of the officer who had, by chance or by design or by Heaven's will, detected her that morning. "If he saw our trail of *qi*, why did he let us through the gate at all? Did we really fool him?"

"Maybe he let us in so we, the vengeance seekers, might lead him to the bigger man behind us, the mightier cause supporting us. That's how they've cracked down on previous uprisings, not by nipping small sparks but by waiting patiently for the roaring flame to show itself so that they could catch all the culprits in one strike. Did your master teach you how to hide the trail of your *qi* within?"

"No." It was the first time Miu Miu had heard of such a thing. All she had learned was that the stronger your power grew, the longer your trail of *qi*, and that nothing should be done to stop that invisible growth lest the foundation be shaken and the accomplishments crumble.

"Father didn't teach me that, either," Tong Ting said, "but I learned it from the book of dark trades. All you need to do to hide the spike of *qi* from within is let yourself sag like an empty bag and cover the nerve hub on top of your scalp with the heart of your palm. Like this," he said, demonstrating, "as if you are putting on a lid, killing your own flame."

"Won't that break my *qi* flow and weaken me?"

"You'd think so, but some rogue warriors—those who have wandered off the straight path—have used this in the past as a way to harness the maximum *qi*, bottling it within and multiplying its potency. It has been known to increase warriors' power to magical proportions, though at the cost, sometimes, of their lives. Suppressing too much *qi* has been known to burst an adept's chest open or blast his head off, though such a warning is hardly for us. We are still novices in our trade and don't have enough *qi* to kill ourselves that way."

"I wouldn't mind dying that way as long as our enemy dies with me." Miu Miu reached her hand up to cover her head, but Tong Ting stopped her.

"No need to do that yet. Perhaps the gate commander is here as part of his duties to guard the emperor. Don't smother your *qi* unless you absolutely need to." He took a deep breath. "I'm going to make my way to the west of the square, close to the river. That will be our way out, even when the city gate is closed. Wait until noon to strike, when all is quiet and the emperor kneels down to pray. When your deed is done, it will be chaos. I will be there waiting for you in the west."

"Farewell," Miu Miu said.

"Don't say that. This is just a temporary parting, not a farewell." Clasping his hands together, Tong Ting offered her a deep bow. Miu Miu returned the gesture in like manner, and they parted.

Miu Miu turned once to catch him glancing back at her. Their eyes clung and held for a few precious long seconds; then she broke the contact and made her way toward the tall tree. The old pine was grandfatherly in all ways possible. Knobby branches reached far and around, providing those standing beneath it with a seamless canopy, shielding them from rain or sun.

Miu Miu arrived at the farthest edge of the ring of worshipers, where a few older folks were piously bowing on the ground, their burning incense sticks driving away the bugs and flies hovering over their sacrificial food: roasted geese and roosters with their heads and feet still intact, laid out in bamboo baskets the pilgrims had carried with them from the country. Her footfalls scarcely disturbed the bent pious heads or the hungry flies.

Miu Miu looked up and located the springy tip of the longest branch. Then her eyes shifted to her final goal: the raised platform where the emperor would see his last noon sun and take his last breath. She could see with her inner eye the perfect arc, imagine the length of her leap and the speed she would need to overcome the wind. She calculated also the force she would need to surprise the man and cut him down with her sword. It was second nature now for her to do this, after all her daily leaps across wide gullies and her jumps up tall trees. Her mind calculated the distance like a clicking abacus, while her heart remained calm like the sea at rest. But her soul had already ignited that little spark, readying itself for the power soon to roar to life. In her mind she could see it all play out: see herself soaring through the dense air like a wingless bird, her arms stretched out, legs trailing, cutting bold strokes upon the canvas of the blue sky.

She waited, remembering what Tong Ting had said about her invisible *qi*, which must be soaring with her ignited inner sparks. She sat down erect, like a Buddhist worshiper, with her legs folded. Then drawing in a long, full breath, she placed the heart of her palm on top of her scalp over the nub where all nerves met. She could not risk being detected and stopped now.

Slowly, she felt a sensation that was alien, something she had never felt before. She sensed herself sinking, thinning, flattening, and cooling, as if she were plummeting down the long, chilling shaft of a deep and hollow well. Weakly, she leaned against the trunk of the tree, wondering if she had done the wrong thing. What would Master Wan have said? Why hadn't he taught her about this?

Her eyelids weighed heavily and she felt

drowsy, as if she had been deprived of sleep for endless nights. She was falling asleep!

Why had Tong Ting not told her that this tactic was so restful, like the soft touch of her mother's old quilt? As she fought to keep herself awake, she began to feel suffocated, as if she had been pushed underwater. She pinched herself, forcing herself to sit straight as she pushed back the cloth covering the sword and its sheath. The touch of the golden hilt seemed to clear her mind.

However dwindled her *qi* had become, it would have to suffice for the act soon to be done.

She glanced to the west, where Tong Ting had said he would wait for her, preparing their route of escape. She trusted his word: the word of her betrothed, the word of a fellow martial artist; words one could count on and lean upon, in need, in chaos. Such a word, once given, was chiseled as firmly as carvings upon a rock.

Leaning back again, Miu Miu tightened her

grip on the sword. It would be any moment now. *Be calm*, she told herself, *be firm*. She had heard those words spoken to her by Father before. In her fading senses he appeared to her in the dark stage of her closed eyes, a vague, blurry figure, not upright but lying over the blood-drenched threshold of their house, his arms flailing in pain. Then a glinting sword swooshed through the air and his hands flew off, one up into the air, the other falling down onto the ground. Miu Miu opened her eyes and the bloody drama vanished.

"Father," she said painfully, feeling as if it were her hands being severed, her heart pierced, her throat swelling with desperate cries. "It is time," she muttered. "It is time that I be your daughter."

Looking up, she saw the royal entourage come into view down the broad boulevard festooned with swinging lanterns and waving banners red as blood.

Nine 劍

THE ROYAL COMPANY choked the streets, causing all in its path to kneel like turtles with their
heads shrunk down and back, and their tails
hidden. Miu Miu counted ten tall horses prancing abreast, each rider carrying a flag; another
ten riders guarded the rear. They formed a tight
square with six other soldiers flanking the
golden carriage drawn by four brown horses
with shiny manes. They came forward and
around the outskirts of the square like horse-
men in a shadow-lantern show. The sight of

that passing carriage was a sinister awakening. "Killer of my father," Miu Miu muttered groggily.

Reality and dreams blended together for a moment. She could smell the mournful stench of her father's blood staining the killer's hands. She could see the crimson blood seeping between the murderer's fingers. Tears flowed from the corners of her eyes, and her muscles began to twitch uncontrollably. She felt the rising urge to grieve for her father, as if the news of his death had just been delivered to her. The twitching became spasms that threatened to unravel her composure and pour out all the sadness that she had kept within. With a jerk, she kept the cries bottled within and pinched her numb cheeks. She bent her fingers backward until they felt like they were about to break. The distant chanting of her master came to her in that moment of anguish and upheaval:

Calm within, calm without;
Wind in and wind out;

Calm up, calm down;
Sea up and sea down.
Let the wind slow,
Let the sea sleep,
Let you, let me, breathe deep.

The verses seemed to part all the clouds and fog, bringing her mind back to clarity and peace.

The carriage came to a stop before the square upon which the emperor was soon to offer his prayer to Heaven. Scores of royal guards formed a ring around the carriage. The white marble pagoda blazed beneath the blue sky as the sun neared its zenith overhead.

Miu Miu's heart started to stutter erratically in her chest. Unwanted thoughts suddenly choked her mind, threatening to undo the fortitude of her vengeance and the sacredness of her pledge: a daughter's pledge, a pledge to forsake her life in the name of her father's.

But did vengeance justify all? Was it an act of selflessness or an act of senselessness? Was she ready to die now? Was it truly to be her last moment?

Miu Miu was suddenly exhausted from the doubt that flooded her mind. Who was she? To whom did she really belong? Were these the questions one asked when one was dying? Was there really a next life? How could anyone know such a thing?

I am dying, Miu Miu thought. *That's why I'm thinking these thoughts. Father*, she asked silently, *do you want me to die for you? Do you, Father?*

Should she walk away from it all, vanish into the forest and live as a wanderer? Or should she leap and kill, living the brief life of an assassin—the same life chosen by many before her? Though she would be dead, her name would live on the face of a wooden plaque for eternity, just like her father's. Yet what was eternity, if she was to die today without issue or heir? Who would stare at her wooden plaque, day in and day out, as she had done to her father's? It would gather dust, staring at her mother's lonely, wrinkled face.

Mother would dust her plaque, even pray to it, watering it with yellow wine on holidays, and on the anniversaries of Miu Miu's birthday and death day. Then her mother would die, and her father's direct line would end. Their home would be torched as a site of misfortune. So would go Father's plaque, Father's name, dying for death's sake rather than living in the celebration of life: a life that Father had seeded with the promise of a prosperous future full of laughing grandchildren to crowd the empty halls his ghost guarded . . . a man who deserved to be worshiped forever as the forefather who had made the finest swords on earth. Glory would prevail in that way, not infamy.

You would want that, wouldn't you, Father? I promise you, with Tong Ting, the good match you made in faith, that your flesh and blood will thrive, no matter its prior shame. I will make certain that our boys come to be the finest swordsmiths, as you once were, and carry on the swordmaking legends of the

Mius. I will make Tong Ting change all the boys' names to Miu. He would not mind, for his own father changed his name in fear of the emperor. See, all living beings are afraid of death? So am I, Father. So am I. Can you hear me?

She felt herself fading and diminishing, and fell forward, bowing, her face to the soil. The square, with all of its magnificence, faded away from her vision, and the ground seemed to tilt as if she were aboard a heaving ship. Yet she felt unafraid, soothed by the sense of being rocked gently in her father's arms. In that imagined swaying, the voice of fate roared inside her head. *Traitor!* it cried. A contorted face rushed at her. It was a watery face, flat of nose, with sharp teeth and bloody mouth.

I am no traitor, Miu Miu told it. *Why should I be bound to die? Why, when I feel such an urge to live?*

Obey that urge, and one cycle of your afterlife will be forfeited.

I fear no punishment. Take two or three of

*my life cycles if you wish. All I desire is this one
with Tong Ting, to bear our children.*

Dare you bargain with fate?

*I dare not bargain with fate. I am pleading
for merciful grace.*

*Grace? You have already been granted
grace, already given mercy!* the voice roared.

*You are just a fabrication. Vanish, you
ghost!* Miu Miu told it, frightened.

The face stretched drum-tight with fury,
then faded away, wrinkling into a cloudy back-
ground against which another figment showed:
her mother, with her features twisted into
knots of agony as a newborn infant's cry
pierced the air.

Mother!

As Miu Miu watched, blood began to drip
from her mother's nose and pour out from
between her thighs.

Was that her birth that fate was showing,
Miu Miu wondered?

In the next scene, she will bleed to death,
said fate. *But she was spared . . . for you. Go,*

unbrave one. Endure.

As the voice faded away, Miu Miu felt strength flooding up from her toes, through the veins of her legs, tingling up her spine, until it reached her scalp.

Why have I wavered? Miu Miu wondered. *Why have I doubted my own intent as a warrior? How could I neglect to save Father's soul from its hellish condemnation?*

"Endure," Miu Miu whispered to herself. When she opened her eyes, her sword was still in her grip and all the faithful citizens of Chang'an were kneeling, awaiting their emperor's prayer as if no time had lapsed. She glanced skyward and saw that the sun was an inch away from high noon.

Miu Miu looked up, conjuring the arc of her pending kill, and saw doves, stark white, and black swallows fly by. One by one, they were shot down, bloody arrows buried deep in their breasts as they plummeted to the square.

No one is to be higher than the sovereign,

by the emperor's decree, Miu Miu remembered. Not even a bird.

The sound of royal bugles blared as high noon finally arrived. The crowd quieted. In the silence that followed, leaves rustled in the breeze and the bleating of goats far away in the distance could be heard.

The emperor climbed down from his carriage, unaided by his men. In his golden gown he slowly ascended the stairs to the platform. He was short and thin, unmanly, an ill-fitting image of the mighty Son of Heaven, which was what emperors proclaimed themselves to be. Facing north, he gingerly kneeled down, tipping his crown forward, a jade-colored incense stick clasped in his hands.

Miu Miu took off into the air like a kite blown aloft by a sudden gale. Soundlessly, the tips of her toes alighted on the bark of that far-reaching branch. It dipped and a leaf or two turned, moved by her motion. Master Wan would have reprimanded her for that imperfection, which caused one or two in the crowd to look up. Tilting her body, she readied herself for the final dive. Before the branch's second dip, Miu Miu flew off again. In flight, she pulled her father's sword out from its sheath, the naked blade shining deep blue in the golden sun. The emperor looked up from his genuflection and caught sight of her.

His hands were quick. Dropping the incense stick, he pulled out a long sword from beneath his gown. His feet were even quicker, nimbly shifting to a tiger's stance. He knocked off his crown with his own hand, revealing a tail of braided hair. A few gasps from the crowd caused more heads to rise.

An emperor was never to be seen without a crown.

Yards from her intended target, Miu Miu was sharply repelled by the hard rim of the man's kung fu aura. It was stronger and much denser than that of her master's: strong enough to suspend her in the air and prevent her from getting any closer to him.

Should I leap away now? Miu Miu wondered. *Should I forfeit? Is escape still possible?*

She blew her *qi* onto the tip of Father's sword, and a spear of blue light dashed forward from the tip, cleaving the force field of the emperor's aura and continuing on toward him. He dodged out of the path of the blue ray, and Miu Miu landed on the platform and thrust her sword, aiming for his left eye. He evaded her thrust narrowly by twisting his neck away. Miu Miu sliced again. The emperor, a surprisingly gifted fighter, bent bonelessly backward like a twig, with his feet rooted, and the sword passed harmlessly over him. Bouncing forward, he dashed his own blade at her with blurry speed, scissoring it at her with calculated gestures in the confusing and confounding tactic of Storm Eye.

Miu Miu countered readily with Spiderweb Ruse, spinning herself out of his path. He zigzagged his nipping sword as she tumbled, web soft, always a thread ahead of him.

All that the crowd witnessed was a whirl of arms and legs and a steely dazzle of the emperor's sword making random cuts and chaotic hacking slashes. The palace soldiers, encircling the square in a noisy clatter, were as beguiled by the display as the citizens.

Miu Miu spiraled up in the air, spider leaping about the platform. She was hoping the emperor would weaken and his initial burst of *qi* wane. But he did not weaken. His sword moved more nimbly and his wrists grew more agile as his Storm Eye churned faster in a widening radius. A few times his blade came dangerously close, but each time she managed to sidle away in a spidery tumble.

As the bout continued, it was Miu Miu who began to weaken as her weariness returned, causing her spider leaps and tumbles to slow. She found it harder and harder to fend off the widening loops of the emperor's Storm Eye.

Desperately, Miu Miu landed on the ground, forfeiting her spidery ruse. Rooting her heels on mother earth, she regathered her *qi*. Sending it to the tip of her sword, she dashed her weapon straight into the iris of the

Storm Eye. Her sword's azure rays, suddenly enlivened, transformed into a sphere that seamlessly encased the entire platform and a little beyond. Amid that brilliant blue, a red cube radiated in defiance, an aberration that came from the emperor's empty carriage perched at the edge of the platform.

Miu Miu drilled her blue sword through the layers of the emperor's Storm Eye and severed his sword in half. As his eyes widened, she plunged Father's sword through his left eye slit. The blade punctured the mask, pierced through the eye, and emerged through the back of his head. He collapsed.

Amazingly, sparkles spewed out of his pierced eye and the emperor was set aflame. Flickering flames rolled down his body, consuming it in a dry death—no gush of blood or spilling of brain or flowing of intestines. Engulfed in fire, his body parts shrank rapidly. His legs disappeared, his arms shortened into shoulder stumps, and his torso turned to ash. He vanished like a magical object into the air.

The only thing left behind was his golden gown, fallen to the ground.

In one second, hatred evaporated and acrimony was gone. Was this how triumph felt, Miu Miu wondered?

She was about to take off when that red cube jarred her senses once more. Why was the royal carriage shielded from the blue rays? Could her real opponent be hiding there, holding Father's red sword? Was the man she had killed an imposter, a warrior set in the emperor's place?

Tumbling three times, Miu Miu landed near the carriage. The curtain was unmoving. The stallions yoked to the carriage stood meekly still under the spell of her blue glare as royal guards rushed to encircle Miu Miu. Arrows were nocked to bows, but the order was given to hold fire. She lifted her hand to part the curtains of the carriage. As she did so, a wave of weakness roiled once more over Miu Miu. Nausea churned her stomach, dizzying her and buckling her knees. The blue sword weighed unbearably heavy in her hands, and her breathing grew labored. In that moment of vulnerability, the curtain rustled, moved by something from within.

With a fiery cry of revenge, Miu Miu cut down the curtain with her sword and charged forward. To her surprise, the interior was empty and the seat vacant. Then the wooden floor of the carriage exploded, and a scrawny man flew up to land in the center of the platform, facing her. In his right hand he gripped the red sword, its blade giving off a crimson glow. He was dressed from head to toe in black, with a metal mask covering his face. He must have hidden beneath the carriage, clinging to the bottom between the four wheels.

"Who are you?" Miu Miu demanded.

"Who are you?" he asked in turn.

"An avenger!"

"Many avengers I have. Name your name, and state your grievance."

"Name *your* name," she retorted.

"How dare you even ask. I am the Son of

Heaven and the ruler of the earth."

"You lie!"

"I have no need to lie. I am the emperor."

"*That* was an emperor," Miu Miu said, pointing to the crown lying on the ground.

"He was a fake, a cousin of mine. I am the one carrying the seal of power," he said, patting the jade seal, the size of a man's palm, strapped to his belt. "You have been fooled, imbecile!"

Imbecile, indeed. She had almost fallen for it.

"Give me your petty name before you fight me," the emperor demanded. "I never drink the blood of an unnamed opponent."

"How pure of you. I am Miu Miu of Goose Village, a swordmaker's daughter. My father, the maker of your red sword, died at your bloody hands."

"Swordmaster Miu. The legendary one. I did not know he had an heir. No matter. I killed him to spare him condemnation from an even higher power."

"Another lie!"

"The truth has been kept from you, it seems," the emperor said with false pity. "The secret that made his swords the finest was the condemned dark craft he practiced. I had him killed to spare him a destined eternity of death. He was to die soon anyway, according to the book of death kept in my possession as the Descended One. Ending his life the way I did allowed him to keep his cycle of nine lives intact. It was a favor with which I blessed him."

Unable to bear another word of this falsehood, Miu Miu drove the blue sword forward with all the power she possessed.

The emperor remained as motionless as a stone statue.

Her sword tip, aimed for his groin, slid off a hidden protective guard. So Tong Ting had been wrong.

He charged with a blurry sequence of quick jabs and sly sweeps known as the Gobi Style, commonly used by desert assassins. Miu Miu deftly countered with the Goose Style tactic:

beaky thrusts and bites, and web-footed plunges. They circled each other, dodging and fencing in an array of ever-changing styles.

"You demonstrate shabby skills," the emperor sneered.

"Eat my sword and die!" Switching to the Mad Monkey style of fighting, Miu Miu leaped up and down, left and right, as if drunk, evading his strikes. Unable to find any weakness, he switched to the Deer Hop tactic, cutting at her with his blade as a deer would, fighting with its antlers, prancing and leaping around her.

He was agile, dodging and attacking, his feet nimble and arms sinuous, all youthful vibrancy when he was supposed to be advanced in years. Was it *he* who practiced the dark arts? Did he take life-lengthening potions or practice age-reversing human sacrifices?

The crowd outside the blue sphere rose to their feet in their suppressed excitement. The emperor shouted, "Put your weapons away. She is mine!" and the guards unnocked their arrows and resheathed their swords.

She switched to Flamingo Foot, standing on her right leg while delivering a forceful kick with her left foot. The emperor evaded her blows by dropping down to the ground in a Python Squirm. Removing his face mask, he hissed his long and slippery tongue at her right foot, coiling it wetly around her ankle in three loops, and pulled back hard with his lassolike tongue, making her lose her balance.

How repulsive his wet tongue felt around her ankle!

The art had originated from the Icy Mountain Style of kung fu, whose hermetic practitioners nailed the tips of their tongues to tree branches and hung from them day and night. As they starved and shed their flesh, they added weights around their ankles. While their tongues lengthened, their masters would beat the stretched tongues with the flat surface of a sword, and later singe them with smoldering chunks of charcoal, creating tongues as tough as leathery whips.

How had the emperor, ensconced in his

palace far from the mountains, have mastered that art? Had he eaten the rare, potent, and sometimes poisonous *ban xia* herb, risking death to grow his tongue? Or had he usurped another's tongue and grafted it onto his own?

His tongue tightened, cutting into her flesh. The pain made her dizzy, and the red dazzle that shone from his sword encompassed her like a hot sun. Her head ached as the sword's red aura singed her clothes, burning holes in places and making her skin blister. All she saw around her was a heaving blur.

Where are you, Tong Ting? Can't you see it's time? I need you now.

The blue light from her sword dimmed beneath the burning red gleam as Miu Miu clung to her weapon, desperately fighting the desire to loosen her fist and let it go, yielding it to the pull of the red sword. As her grip began to loosen and her knees weaken, and she felt herself falling to the ground, a shadow rose up from the western corner of the square and soared into the battle zone. It was Tong Ting, with dagger in hand, dashing straight for the emperor's red sword. With a clash of sparking light, Tong Ting's dagger punctured the rim of the red glare, then crumbled into dust inches before reaching the emperor's sword.

Perturbed by Tong Ting's intrusion, the emperor uncoiled his tongue and pulled it back into his mouth, leaving Miu Miu a limp tangle on the ground, and turned to face the new threat, just in time to see Tong Ting hurling three more flying daggers at him. The emperor stood still, letting the daggers fly unimpeded at him. Just before they would have struck him, all the daggers fell like swatted mosquitoes, dropping meekly at his feet.

"Village scoundrel, come closer if you dare," the emperor taunted. "Constraint and containment, my boy, something you will likely never know. Come near—I am famished. I shall feast this night on your chewy little dragon meat, washed down with aged *mai tao* liquor. Even an aloof one could not have wished for more." The emperor flicked his tongue over his lips as if to savor the delicacy to come. As he levered the tip of his red sword at Tong Ting, the red light enlarged its rim.

Weaponless now, Tong Ting sucked in his lungs, flattened his belly, and called on the full reserve of his remaining *qi*. The roots of his power had been planted within long ago by his father's *qi gong*. The emperor was right to identify Tong Ting with the dragon. His father's learning had originated from a crippled hermit who lived on the shores of Hai Long Jiang, Black Dragon River, where dragons were said to still swim in the deep waters. Dragon worshipers risked their lives, sinking down to the frozen floor of the river to be near the black dragon and harvest trickles of the dragon's blood that seeped up through the cracks in the ancient sediment.

Tong Ting's father had resorted to the dark trade in desperation, trying to fight evil with evil after he and all his offspring had been condemned to death. The decree was still in effect. This dark art had been duly passed on to Tong Ting, his only son.

At his calling, Tong Ting's power roared forth in one punishing spurt. As it fanned out from his core, he felt the chilling flow of the dragon's blood trickle out. His eyes rolled back in their sockets, and his irises and pupils flashed white as his face turned black and scaly. Opening his mouth, he spewed out dark flames that pierced the red glare, cutting it in half.

The emperor opened his own mouth in turn and began to suck in Tong Ting's black flames, swallowing them all until Tong Ting was empty and there was no more. With a great roar, the emperor shot the blackness back at Tong Ting.

"A half dragon is no dragon!" the emperor said scornfully. "I am the red dragon of the eastern sea!"

Singed and drained of power, screaming with pain, Tong Ting crawled to where Miu Miu lay.

"Send them to the royal cookhouse," the emperor commanded his men, sheathing his red sword. "And take that blue sword as well."

The guards cautiously approached Tong

Ting and Miu Miu, still wary of their power.

A warrior is never without his last resort, Tong Ting thought. His was a final black flame he blew out at the guards. Dark fire licked at the faces and bodies of the royal vultures, and they fled in fear.

"What folly." The emperor chuckled scornfully. "You useless guards can take them now—he is empty."

As the guards drew near once more, Tong Ting reached out a shaky hand and grasped the blue sword, pulling it from Miu Miu's grip.

Blue is the more vital of the pair, Tong Ting remembered his father saying to him. *Blue is the path*. But he knew not how to call on the blue sword's deadliest power. All he remembered was his father's other words about the legendary sword: *In you, with it, all foes will fade*.

Opening his mouth wide, Tong Ting raised the sword high and thrust the blue sword's fierce tip into his own mouth. He jammed it painfully down his throat, into his guts, until he had swallowed half the blade. When the tip of the sword reached the pit of belly, his *dun-tien*, he gagged and a deep nausea rose within him. Pain cut him from inside and he felt penetrated and sliced.

Death is dawning, Tong Ting thought, *and I am ready.* But slowly, within him, he felt the sharpness of the blade soften and bend. Pain receded as if soothed by a balmy herb, and he began to glow with blue light. It poured out of his body with eerie brilliance from his eyes and mouth, his ears and nose, his back and chest, making the soldiers flee like headless ghosts and the crowd scream and run in fright.

The emperor shot out his tongue again to ensnare them but was repelled in turn by the blue light. Tong Ting picked up Miu Miu in his arms and held her tight against his chest.

Roaring, the emperor opened his mouth and shot a great red flame at them. Tong Ting felt his heart sink and his mind lament as it reached out to engulf them. Clutching Miu Miu close to his heart, he waited to be undone by the emperor, and felt comforted by Miu Miu's light body resting peacefully in his arms. "Together forever," he murmured to her.

Just before the emperor's flame touched them, Tong Ting felt his heart suddenly expand, as if its chambers were being filled with a jostle of new life. He felt his strength gaining and his will renewing itself. Slowly he felt himself pulled upward, not by an outward force but by inner vigor. He rose, up and away from the red flame, ascending gently like a kite taking flight. His foe's long tongue shot after him again to wrest them down, but was repelled by an invisible force that made it fall to the ground with a thud.

Tong Ting flew higher and even higher, lifted away from the square, above the pagoda, into a blue sky with the sword still embedded in him, giving him a warmth and a joy he had not known before. The air thinned and the sun grew warmer as they glided over the encircling city walls. They floated over green farmlands and thick forests through the endless sapphire sky.

Tong Ting felt like a wingless bird, free and weightless, as they flew farther west.

When he saw that they had gone far enough away from the inner city, Tong Ting thought, *Descend, blue sword,* and descend they did. Before long they landed in a wild grove of green bamboo. Parting the swaying trees, he found a grassy patch to lay Miu Miu down on; then, lying beside her, he carefully pulled the blue sword out from his throat. He expected pain and blood, but there was no blood, no pain.

Pressing his lips to the handle, he thanked the sword in silence.

Ten 劍

THAT NIGHT, TONG TING snuck back to Willow Village with Miu Miu on his back. Wu Ting, his father—or Wu Lu, as he was now known—met him at the door still wearing the black robe of his professional mourner's garb. Their home was a low hut topped by a thatched roof and a stout smokestack. Wu Ting had a gaunt face with sunken cheeks, a dripping nose, and red eyes befitting a sorrowful funeral weeper for hire. He had just returned from a day's job of weeping for a rich man who had choked to death on a chicken bone. Even at the summer solstice people died and had to be buried.

Tong Ting's mother had died long ago after a famine. Since there was no woman's touch, the household was chaotic, with agitated roosters and hens dashing here and there. A week's worth of dirty dishes was piled atop the brick stove, and the unswept earthen floor had chicken droppings, rice straw, and corn husks strewn all over.

Wu Ting rushed them in, surprised by the stranger on his son's back, and closed the shaky door quickly behind them to keep out his neighbors' spying eyes.

"Something terrible has happened," Tong Ting told him, laying Miu Miu on his narrow wooden bed, which leaned against the west wall of the one-room hut. Breathlessly he recounted the day's heroic events.

Wu Ting squatted by Miu Miu, examining her and shaking his head. "I always knew this day would come. You should have asked for help; we could have done it together. Now look at her, all wounded and weakened. How can I face my master when we meet again in the next realm?"

"Is there a cure, any cure?" Tong Ting asked, hoping that his father, a man of many skills and trades, would be able to whip out a rare herb or grind some expedient powder as he always did when Tong Ting suffered a cold or a run of fever.

"Bleeding blisters around her ankles, swollen legs, yellowing of skin," Wu Ting said, muttering to himself all of Miu Miu's symptoms. Looking up at Tong Ting, he barked, "Get my pillow."

Tong Ting rushed to his father's bed, leaning against the opposite wall, and picked up the pillow. Hidden inside it was a thick book containing his father's handwritten notes on rare diseases and afflictions that he had encountered or heard from others. Hurriedly, Wu Ting opened the book to a page on snake-bites.

"It matches all the symptoms of yellow

python poisoning," he finally said.

"What is that?" Tong Ting asked.

"It comes from the venom of a yellow python found in the water forest. The emperor must have carried the poison in his tongue."

"Will she die?"

"Worse. The blisters will burst and yellow pus will ooze. When the oozing stops, her skin will dry and yellow scales will appear; her tongue will fork and her limbs will wither as she slowly transforms into a wormlike creature that will be ravaged with a lust to inflict upon others what was inflicted upon her. She herself will be nearly indestructible." Turning the page, Wu Ting read on. "The emperor has used this poison on ten occasions that I know of, the last time three years ago on Li Po, a rebellious poet. Now his entire town has been enclosed with tall walls and quarantined, with all the sickened townsfolk squirming and multiplying within."

"That can't happen to her, Father! She is your master's only offspring, to be my bride!"

"Calm yourself, son. You said she was a gifted martial artist."

Ting Tong nodded.

"Who taught her?"

"The head monk of Goose Village."

"Master Wan?"

"You know him?"

"He is a saintly man who saved not only the Miu family but us as well, after her father's murder."

"But how can he help Miu Miu's illness now?"

"As a martial warrior yourself, you should know better. *Zai sheng*—born again. Do you know what that is?"

Tong Ting shook his head.

"Rebirth. That is the only cure for her: to empty her dirtied blood and marrow and refill it anew. Her kung fu master will know the basic constituents of her living fluids, and what to refill her veins with. Before a master can teach a student, he must know what she is made of. We must bring her back to Goose

Village at once. You carry her and I will guard you. We will depart at midnight."

For the next seven days, Tong Ting carried Miu Miu on his back, hurrying from one village to another, passing through mountainous ranges and untamed wilderness. Miu Miu was delusional and, at times, delirious. Her skin turned jaundiced, clammy and hot during the day, cold at night. She shivered at intervals and was stiff at other times. But Tong Ting was comforted greatly by the fact that his father was always ahead of him, scouting out the safest path, which was not always the easiest route. They stayed away from the main roads, which were flooded with imperial guards hunting down the two fugitives. The army's presence was evidenced by ominous royal flags that hung limply at each village and township, as far as a hundred miles distant from the capital.

One night, when Wu Ting ventured into a southern village to buy Miu Miu some ginseng to lessen her fever, he was nearly caught by the village sheriff after the man was tipped off by the herbalist, who had noted Wu Ting's northern accent.

That night, father and son didn't sleep a wink or stop to rest as they retreated into the mountains where tigers roamed and wolves howled. The fever was temporarily curtailed; but left uncured, Miu Miu's disease would slowly overtake her.

When exhaustion overcame him, Tong Ting would reluctantly let his father carry her while he stopped to take a drink from a nearby river and wash Miu Miu's face, scooping the fresh water into her mouth. He tried feeding Miu Miu some of the dried food his father had packed, but Miu Miu spewed it back up. Tong Ting ran on with her on his back until the moon set and the night grew too dark to continue. Only then did he seek refuge under a tree, slipping into exhausted slumber while holding Miu Miu tightly in his arms.

As days wore on and nights passed, the girl who had been so slim and light began to weigh upon him like the heavy rock slabs he used to carry on his shoulders when he'd labored to build rich men's houses in the inner city of Chang'an. No matter the martial arts lessons that had made his legs strong or the labor that had toughened his muscles, the road began to feel steep when it was flat, and bumpy when it was smooth. His iron feet, which had passed the test of smoldering coals and heated sand, began to feel as thin and tender as silk. But he dragged himself onward.

"Where am I?" Miu Miu would sometimes murmur feverishly, her parched lips burning and dry.

"You are going home," Tong Ting would answer her.

"Why am I going home? I can't go home."

"To be cured. To rest."

"I've shamed Mother . . . Father . . . the village elder."

"You've made me proud."

"I have failed," she would mutter until she drifted off again.

Although Miu Miu could not digest dried food, she could eat fruit. Tong Ting fed her three times a day and once during the night. While resting, he leaned her against a hill, a tree, or a bale of hay, waiting for the stars to shine again or the sun to rise once more. He fetched fresh water from nearby brooks to soothe her throat and picked the ripest fruits— pungent lychee, sweet longan, and yellow loquats from the wild orchards—chewed them into pulp, and fed them slowly into her mouth, bit by tiny bit, so that she would not choke.

Three days before reaching Goose Village, their last hurdle loomed before them: the infamous Bridge Town whose foul repute Wu Ting had long heard of from his apprentice days, when the dwarf lord's father had still been alive. This far south, away from the capital city, the emperor and his palace were forgotten. The south was where roguish provinces still held tight to their quaint traditions and customs, and where rebels, thieves, and warlords gathered. The emperor was usually content as long as annual taxes were levied and collected, and trouble remained distant. But what Wu Ting observed from a nearby hill alarmed him.

The royal flags, decorated with red dragons, flew from the headstone of every bridge. Soldiers were everywhere, their armor gleaming, helmets shining, sharp spears reflecting the warm sun.

Wu Ting paid a discreet visit to an upriver undertaker. There he found poor men's coffins, the reusable kind that one could rent for a funeral procession but not the real burial. Even better, there were convenient choices of a coffin with wheels as well as a coffin built on a raft. It was the latter he rented, spending his last penny. Hiding both Miu Miu and his son snugly in the single coffin, he poled it out during the morning rush when the river was busiest. In his loud, professional mourner's voice, he cried for the dead on board.

Superstitious folk cursed him, spitting his way while poling frantically away, so as not to bump into the unfortunate raft, believing that misfortune could rub off onto them. Even the river patrollers cruising with the pompous soldiers pinched their noses and cursed loudly at him to pole quickly on.

The round moon followed them southward, alternating with the hot sun as they traveled to their destination. On Tong Ting's back was his destiny; resting on his shoulders was his fate. So Tong Ting ran, heading south to Goose Village, journeying deep down into the country, away from his own familiar land. Willow Village was a memory he had left far behind as the southern stars shone bright, guiding his way, and the southern sun glared upon their path by day.

On the seventh day they arrived at their destination. "Miu Miu is sickened with illness," Wu Ting told his son. "Her presence must not taint the temple. Take her to her mother's home while I seek Master Wan's help." Pointing his son to the right direction, he sent him on the final stretch of his journey.

At noon Tong Ting came across an erect rock carved with the words GOOSE VILLAGE. His knees quivered and he almost collapsed with the weight of Miu Miu on his back, but he firmed his joints and leaned for a moment against the rock.

So near.

He wanted to shout his joy to the heavens, to share his relief with his sleeping bride. Leaning Miu Miu against the rock, he went to the nearby brook. Wetting his sleeves, he gently washed her face and neck, lightly patting all the scattered blisters darkened with road dust. She sighed at the soothing relief and his heart expanded with love and a touch of triumph and pride.

He washed his own blistered feet, then dipped his head under the water and gave it a thorough scrubbing. When he came up, he saw a few goose eggs lying near the river bed. Picking one up, he cracked it on his forehead and slurped it all in one gulp.

So this was Goose Village, with eggs everywhere along the river, waiting to be hatched.

Wiping the dripping yolk from his lips, he caught a glimpse of his own reflection in the wavering brook.

I am ready to meet the mama of my bride, he thought. *I am ready for the wedding.*

With that blushing thought, Tong Ting picked up Miu Miu once again and headed into the village.

Eleven 劍

UNTENDED GEESE FLOCKED to him, quacking loudly as soon as Tong Ting entered the village. Some pecked at his bare feet, others at his calves. Tong Ting danced around them with Miu Miu heavy on his back, dodging and kicking, which only stirred them to a fiercer assault.

Goose-herding boys leaped down, one by one, from the leafy persimmon tree they had been perched on. "What is your business coming to Goose Village, stranger?" the head boy, a flat-faced youngster, inquired, whipping his long bamboo pole at Tong Ting, its wet tip dripping with mud.

"It is Miu Miu I am carrying. I am bringing her home from the capital city. Please let me through."

"The widow's daughter?" the boy said, frowning. "Isn't she *gui tian* already?" The phrase meant "returning to Heaven."

"No, she is still alive. Come, make way for me."

"We aren't supposed to let anyone through without the elder's permission."

"She is dying—can't you see?" Tong Ting said tightly.

"She is already dead. Her plaque is on the heroes' table in the village temple."

"Come here. I have a ripe persimmon in my pocket," Tong Ting coaxed. Persimmon fruit did not ripen on trees. It usually took up to a month under a thick blanket to soften one enough to eat.

As soon as the boy was within reach, Tong

Ting freed one hand and grabbed his bony neck. "Now tell your geese to make way or I will break your neck like a twig."

He gave the boy a little squeeze, and the rascal did as he was told. At his sharp whistle, the geese disentangled themselves from Tong Ting's ankles, waddling away.

Over the stone bridge, by a quiet brook, was Miu Miu's ancestral home.

"Mother of Miu Miu!" Tong Ting shouted from the front gate. The wooden entry had been painted black. On its frame, a poem was inscribed in the finest calligraphy, proclaiming the essence of the house and its *feng shui*—its wind-and-water relation to its surroundings.

Mountain hues greet all seasons bright;
River sounds soothe all year round.

The vertical strokes of the calligraphy were staunch but not hard, the horizontal hooks supple but not soft. Tong Ting wondered if it was the handwriting of the master swordmaker himself. How he wished he were here to meet the legendary artisan and to claim his bride, rather than delivering a sick daughter back to her home.

"Village widow, a stranger has come to your door with Miu Miu on his back," the goose boy, who had followed Tong Ting, shouted in his squeaky voice, while pounding his fist on the gate, as three of his friends crowded around behind him.

A woman opened the gate door a crack, giving Tong Ting a glimpse of a black dress, black shoes, and a beautiful oval face. She didn't greet him right away or appear eager to look at her daughter. She waved her handkerchief to chase the goose boys away, scolding, "Shoo, you scoundrels! Go away!"

"Lonesome widow of Goose Village," the head boy sang, "where all men can stop by for a nap."

"You son of a whore, go away!" Snatching up some rocks, she threw them at the boys. They scattered away to climb back up the persimmon trees and perch on their branches like a flock of dark sparrows.

Taking a brief look at Miu Miu, she beckoned Tong Ting to come in. Latching the black gate, she led him across a stone-paved front yard past stout peach trees and a well, leading him not into the central hall of her home but to a stone-walled shed with an earthen smokestack on its roof, detached from the main house.

She flung open the door, startling a black dog napping on a bamboo daybed. *It must be the swordmaker's workshop,* Tong Ting thought. Hammers leaned against the wall. Nearby sat an old stove still piled with half-burned chunks of coal. Next to the stove lay a warped bellows whose handle his own father must have pushed and pulled day and night, building a pure flame for his master.

"Out you go, foolish puppy." Dragging the dog off the bed, she pushed it out the door. "Put her down here," she said, pointing at the daybed. "Her father used to nap here. Sometimes when working late, he would spend the night here. It was to be her deathbed. I prepared it for her the day she left. Now look at her favorite mat, all wrinkled and covered with dog hair." She clucked her tongue, dusting away the hair.

When she was done, Tong Ting carefully laid Miu Miu down. Her weight settled onto the thin bamboo mat with a creak. Her face was as pale as the ashes in the stove. Her cheeks were creased with wrinkles from being pressed against Tong Ting's shirt, her lips were dried and chapped, and her eyes shut in deep sleep. Had it not been for the shallow rise and fall of her chest, one would have thought her dead, ready for a coffin. Patches on her neck were purpled with blisters, with more of the same on her hands and feet.

"Did she kill the emperor?" Miu Miu's mother demanded.

"I carried her for seven days and nights on end so that she could be saved, and all you are concerned about is whether she killed the enemy."

"Who are you to talk to me like this?"

"I am Tong Ting of Cicada Village, the only son of your husband's apprentice. The bearer of—"

"A jade necklace."

"Yes." Eagerly, Tong Ting fished it out and showed it to her.

She barely glanced at the necklace. "Did she kill that devil emperor?" she asked again.

"No, she didn't, because she couldn't. The enemy was powerful and his fighting art peerless. By a miracle the legend's blue sword saved us, flying us beyond danger. She has survived the long journey. She could live, with Master Wan's help."

"What is the use?" the woman asked bitterly. "It is better if she died."

"You want your own daughter, your only child, to die?"

"The sooner, the better."

Twelve

MIU MIU DREAMED of being engulfed by heat, as if the sun had directed its flames upon her and no one else. She was shrinking and shriveling, bit by bit, with the burning blue sky above and the crackling dry earth below. All things in nature wore an ashen shawl of death as cicadas eulogized the withered flowers and birds sang a dirge for the dying blossoms, lamenting their own fate as well. Dried bamboo groves groaned and crackled beneath the hot gusting wind, and there was thirst, such thirst, as if the land had been scourged by a thousand-year drought. Her flesh was drying, her tongue shrinking, her throat cracking as the dry earth was opened, seam by seam. The only thing growing was a fierce thirst, as if she had swallowed a sea of salt, and that salt consumed her now, soaking her in brine, dissolving her as maggots crawled over her limbs.

The thirst replaced all her desires save for the need to vomit, to gulp deep and dredge her entrails clean. Nights had passed, marked only by the blinking stars and, occasionally, a stoic moon. It made no difference: day or night, there was only darkness.

Her dreams gave way to the feeling of a cold bamboo mat beneath her. On the bare skin of her chest was the scent of green lotus leaf. On her forehead was a bar of coolness . . . no, chilliness, as if someone had placed icicles there. The coldness pinched her temples, clearing the cloudiness from her head and dissipating the waves of heat rising from within.

Miu Miu opened her eyes and saw a blurry

vision of her mother dipping a linen cloth into a pail and wringing it out. Next to her stood a young man, tall and somber. She could not recall having met him. Beyond those two faces were familiar objects from her girlhood—the slanting ceiling darkened with soot, the peeling wall paint, the window upon whose sill sat a statue of Buddha. Above her was a skylight through which rays of the sun shone in by day and moonbeams by night.

I am home, she thought. That discovery startled her, waking her further. *Why am I home? Wasn't I supposed to do something? What was it that I was to accomplish?* Whatever it was, it was something heavy that weighed upon her weakened heart.

Had she failed her mother? Had she somehow failed her many score uncles and aunts and cousins? Was she only homesick and dreaming she was here?

As her senses cleared further, she saw two more figures nearby: a tall man, an utter stranger, and the familiar figure of her master.

What was Master Wan doing here, bending over her, feeding her spoonfuls of bitter broth that made her mind go dark and head dizzy again? Bitterness roiled deep within her and sent chills down her spine, making her shiver all over. She began to retch, and continued doing so until it was only saliva coming up, but the urge to vomit persisted. She felt her fingertips pricked by a slight pain, and a jarring sensation as if her wrists were being slit.

"*Huan xue,*" she heard Master Wan mutter. Changing blood? Why? What was wrong with her blood? Then all her thoughts and senses ceased. Even her heartbeat, the only motion still tangible to her, faded into a tunnel, deep and cold, a whirling that sucked her inward.

When she came to, days had passed. It was Mother's fuzzy profile Miu Miu first saw when she opened her eyes again. She knew she was resting on Father's old daybed in the work shed, and the sun was shining through the skylight, shaded by the tallest lychee branch, which dipped heavy with its thorned and crimson fruit.

"Mother, what has happened to me?" Miu Miu rasped weakly.

"You were poisoned."

"Am I well now?"

"Thanks to Master Wan." Mother nodded, then frowned.

"Why do you look troubled?"

"I'd rather a *si gui*"—a death ghost—"had taken you."

"Why, Mother?" Reaching out, she feebly grasped her mother's hand and felt her squeeze back.

Wrinkles of worry framed her mother's eyes, and dark bags of sleeplessness pouched the skin beneath. "You know why."

The haze slowly faded away as Miu Miu remembered. "But I fought till the very last moment. I fought until I was overpowered by the emperor, Mother. I did, really." She tried to push herself up on her elbow, but dizziness overcame her and she dropped back onto the daybed.

"It is not enough. Either you kill the emperor and are a hero, or you die avenging your father. Anything else and you shame me, your father, and the entire village. There is no in between. It was what I pledged to the elder and what he expected of you."

"I would have died but for Father's sword. Maybe it was Father's wish that we live, Tong Ting and I, to carry on his glory in the children that we bear and rear, and their children afterward. Where is my Tong Ting?"

"You are mad!" Mother cried, covering Miu Miu's mouth.

"But I am not," Miu Miu said, pushing her hand away. "I saw Father, his bleeding self. His face was much like mine: long, with a straight nose, high arcing brows, a square jaw—"

"You make no sense. If you tell them this talk of seeing your father's ghost, they will bury you by sunset," Mother said harshly, casting a glance at the shut door.

"Who are 'they'?"

"The Miu clansmen: your uncles, your

cousins. Had it not been for your gallant groom, they would have taken you days ago, fever or no fever."

"Tong Ting?"

"Yes."

"What are my clansmen here for?"

"To enforce the clan rule, to take you to Goose Cliff."

"For beheading?"

Mother nodded, the creases of her deep frown aging her by a decade.

"Curse my clansmen!" Miu Miu cried.

Mother slapped Miu Miu across the face, the first time she had ever done so. The force stung daughter and mother alike and sent Miu Miu halfway off the daybed. In silence Miu Miu held her stinging cheek.

"Please, Miu Miu. Please don't tell anything about seeing Father. That is cowardice and a lie." Pushing Miu Miu's hand away, she kissed the burning red mark her own hand had made. Clasping Miu Miu's hands in hers, she doubled them against her cheek. Slowly, tears seeped between their entwined fingers. "Miu Miu, I am sorry . . . I should never have urged you to take up this task in the first place."

"Open the door or we will break it down!" a coarse voice shouted through the window. The cries of others no less indignant followed the shouted demand.

"You try and you will see blood." It was Tong Ting's voice Miu Miu heard. She stood up and was overcome for a moment by a dizzy spell. When it passed, she smoothed her blouse and combed her fingers through her hair. "Let me out. Let me see my clansmen."

"They will take you," her mother said starkly.

"Let them take me. I am a Miu, a cursed Miu. So I shall die a cursed Miu. What a glorious name it is, what a loving clan, Miu!" Walking out of the shed, she unlatched the wooden gate door and saw a siege outside. Her house was surrounded by the angry men of Goose Village: able-bodied farmers, fishermen, carpenters, and mountain men. Men of all trades. Men who were her uncles and cousins. Men carrying long swords, short daggers, bows and arrows, ropes, and fighting sticks. They were scattered on the ground and on the wall tops.

On the lychee branches hung the clan children, the Mius of the future, furiously shouting to have the cursed coward scourged and her sin punished.

Tong Ting, wearing nothing but his trousers, stood in front of the gate, facing the looming dark heads surrounding him, his hands gripping the blue sword. Its blade caught the brilliant glare of the morning sun, ready to strike those who dared come near.

The opening of the door caused Tong Ting to turn toward Miu Miu in surprise. In that moment of vulnerability, a shadow leaped off a nearby persimmon tree. Snatching the blue sword away from Tong Ting, he delivered a forceful punch to her defender's forehead. With a groan of surprise and pain, Tong Ting crashed back into Miu Miu's arms, sending them both crashing down on the ground.

The man who had leaped from the tree was none other than Miu Miu's monk, Master Wan, a thin old man with broad shoulders and bright eyes gleaming beneath bushy eyebrows. The punch he had delivered was merely a subduing strike to keep Tong Ting from battling the angry mob. The head monk stood before the crowd, which was eager to kill, angry beyond reason, waving their weapons, ready for blood.

"There will be no killing this hour or the next!" the monk's deep voice rang out. "The village law says that no matter how gravely one has sinned, he is to be given a trial. Execution without a trial would be contrary to our beliefs."

"Why do you interfere?" someone shouted angrily.

"Miu Miu has been to my temple for prayer. She is a child of our faith, a blossom of the Buddhist tree, a fatherless Miu daughter whose father, may I remind you, has done us much honor."

A carpenter with a shining ax, his eyes fixed intently on Miu Miu, tried to sneak through the cracks of the crowd past the monk. In a forceful side blow, the monk buried his elbow in the man's throat, knocking him back against a peach tree.

"I will cut the next challenger's toes off with this ax," the monk said, two weapons in his hands now. "Who wishes to try next?"

There were no takers.

"Rope them together and carry them to the carriage," Master Wan ordered. "Any dereliction and I shall make good the punishment. Village law should be equally applied, may it be for the sinners or you, the innocents."

Miu Miu felt her hands being bound by the same rope that tied Tong Ting's wrists. There was a time for fighting and a time for submission. She had been Master Wan's pupil for most of her life: She chose now to obey her master's cues.

The carriage was mule drawn, and the road to the ancestral hall bumpy. The jerky ride made Miu Miu nauseous. En route to their destination, she fainted again, unaware of the village children who threw rocks at them or the sound of her mother's sobs.

Thirteen 劍

MIU MIU'S TRIAL later that day was merely ceremonial, with only the scrawny village elder presiding over it. Miu Miu and Tong Ting were roped to a central column in the crowded village hall, upon which were nailed their planks of sins. Tong Ting was still unconscious from the monk's subduing blow.

The elder knocked his walking cane against the toe of the stone statue of his forefather and told the crowd first about the delinquent taxes and village levies that some in attendance owed him as the oldest lineal heir of the village's original founding family. Those named—a carpenter, a cow farmer, and a fisherman—ducked their heads in shame. All raised their hands in a pledge to pay as soon as they were able. The fisherman received the most severe tongue-lashing for failing to divide up the wedding fee he had gotten by marrying off a stepdaughter.

Everything here cost money, the elder said. And debt was worse than death, he added, as if pronouncing an exalted truth. Only after he had put away his abacus did he come to the subject of the trial. He didn't even bother to recount the facts, though he did pointedly mention that Miu Miu's mother had indeed bought, for five barrels of rice, the right for Miu Miu to act in the position of a son to avenge her father. Those rights were not usually for sale, he noted, but the mother had pleaded, and he could not stand a widow's tears. He paused before addressing Miu Miu with the summation of her sins.

"You know well the village canons," the

scrawny elder said. "When you take on such a pledge, you kill your enemy or you die under your foe's sword. We have such a stringent rule because we believe that only by death of one or the other may our ancestors be redeemed to ascend onto a higher realm. The purpose of vengeance is not to assuage a living hatred but to fulfill the wishes of the dead. Shame is on the living, those who forgo their pledge."

"What is the shame of living, of wanting to live?" Miu Miu asked angrily.

"What is the shame?" the elder fumed. "The shame lies in not killing your enemy, that devil emperor who killed your father. The shame lies in being spared by the evil one who darkened our clan's name and our village's reputation. That is the shame! That is cowardice and ingloriousness, a bad example for all youngsters to see. If you had guts, you should have stabbed your own chest with your father's sword after you shamelessly escaped from death, from true glory.

"When you returned, I thought you would

just die quietly. But no, Monk Wan had to intervene and cure you. I let him do it with impunity so that you could face a just trial, so you could see your failure and face the consequences." He speared Miu Miu with his dark eyes. "Now, what do you have to say for your shameful self?"

"I fought with my life, with my last ounce of strength. I would have willingly died there, but my father's sword saved us," Miu Miu said.

"Was it really your father's sword that saved you? That sounds like a fairy tale to me," the elder said sneeringly. "Or did the emperor let you go so that you could lead him to us, letting you rat out the entire Miu clan and implicate Goose Village for treason and subversion?"

"I speak the truth about the sword's wonder. In its presence, I even saw my father's face, just before I battled the emperor. Father wanted me to live. He didn't want me to die for him. There is no truth in what you say. The dead cannot be redeemed by the sacrifice of the living. If you hang me for adhering to a lie, you should be hanged yourself!"

"How dare you speak such blasphemy!" the elder shouted. "How dare you use the lie of your father's ghost to frighten us. You deserve the worst death."

"Mother!" Miu Miu cried. "Take me away from here. Don't let them hang me!" She tried to free herself from the ropes, but her weakness made her helpless.

Her mother rushed to Miu Miu's side from where she had been sitting in the back row reserved for women. "Tell him you will get well, recover, and take on the task again," she urged, shaking Miu Miu's shoulder. "Tell them—"

"Mother, I don't want to take up the task again. It's all a lie. Father wants me to live. . . . "

Her mother slapped her across her face, stunning Miu Miu into a shocked daze. Some of the women in the back were weeping. Two stood to speak in her defense but were quieted by their husbands, who ridiculed them for their ignorance of worldly matters.

It took the elder three knocks of his cane to quiet the crowd and pass his judgment. "Since the widow's daughter has not only failed to honor her pledge but also spoken blasphemy, I am left with no choice but to deliver the harshest sentence upon her, not just in the name of justice but to also teach all women a vital lesson: to be content with their inferiority and never meddle in the affairs of men. Miu Miu is to be beheaded in the morning."

As an afterthought, he passed the same sentence on Tong Ting, whom he accused of aiding Miu Miu in her shameful escape from her filial responsibility. "And you," he said, pointing his cane at Miu Miu's mother. "I could have punished you for allowing your daughter to take on such a path. But two deaths are enough for the day, and you will have no more daughters to misguide or mislead anyway."

Mother crawled to the elder's knees. "You said two deaths will be enough for the day.

May I not die in my daughter's stead? Let her live. After all, I was the one who set her on the path. When I die, she will have no one to lead her astray anymore. I am an evil woman, a cursed one, bringing death to all surrounding me: first my husband, then my daughter and her betrothed. You should behead me and rid the Mius of this misfortune for good."

"You may die, if you so choose," said the elder indifferently. "But not in lieu of your daughter."

"Her punishment will kill me: I will die from sorrow and regret. Cannot my willing death be worth anything? Can I trade it in any way to lessen her sentence?"

After quiet deliberation, the elder nodded. "There is a way, a good way. I will make another precedent for you just this once, so that the mothers of the village in the back row can see what is to befall them if they follow in your path."

"I am grateful," Mother said tearfully, her head bowed down at his feet.

"But it will cost you."

"No matter," Mother murmured. "What do you desire?"

The elder plucked his abacus. "Half your estate."

"Take the entire estate. We will all be gone. I only beg to be allowed to bury my husband's plaque in our front yard, so that he will have a home always."

The elder frowned. "That will ruin all the good *feng shui* of the house. That cannot be done."

"Then in the corner of our backyard, near the work shed."

"Granted," the elder said. "The entire estate shall go to me for safekeeping in perpetuity." Zealous villagers shouted their approval, waking their napping neighbors, who had become bored by the proceedings.

"What will you grant me then?" Miu Miu's mother asked meekly.

"The way of the rope—which you should have long ago chosen. And I will grant the dead man's brew for your daughter and her intended, so that when the swords strike their necks tomorrow, they will feel no pain or sorrow."

Drawing in a deep breath, Miu Miu's mother nodded in agreement.

"All those in favor of the above verdict, throw in your bamboo sticks now or speak nevermore on this matter again!" the elder called out. Each village household had been given a bamboo stick for the vote. One tossed stick was one vote in favor. An exact count was rarely warranted—it was usually unanimous. Such was the spirit of Goose Village. All quacked the same quack.

Casually and carelessly, the villagers tossed in their sticks, some into the designated bamboo container, others onto the stage, barely missing Miu Miu and Tong Ting.

"Can we go home now?" asked one villager impatiently.

"Not yet, Farmer Dong. Your rice seedlings can wait and the geese will lay eggs without you. Now we have to fulfill our part of the grant. Bring out the dead man's brew."

A village militiaman disappeared from the hall and returned with a dusty jar. Two more joined him on the stage. Pulling back Miu Miu's head by her long hair, they poured the liquor down her throat.

"No!" Miu Miu screamed and sputtered, but its effects were quick. Within seconds, her head dipped and her legs gave way. Only the ropes binding her to the column kept her from collapsing onto the stage. When they gave Tong Ting the brew, his only sign of protest was a groan and a choking sound as he coughed. Then he sagged as limply as before.

Miu Miu's mother was soothed by the thought that they would be in deep sleep until their heads were severed. Her daughter would die without pain, in the company of her destined groom, and the two souls would fly up to the sky together.

She walked across the stage to where a rope was tied and secured from a beam by the same militiamen who had fetched the brew for her daughter. She stepped up onto a stool that would be duly kicked out by a hangman come the morrow. Catching the wide noose with her hand, she pulled it over her head and fastened it around her neck. Not bad, this way of the rope, the privilege of widows. She didn't even shake: It felt right. She felt neither regret nor sadness. She was ready to die with Miu Miu and her groom. Widowhood had long outlived its usefulness.

Fourteen

VIGIL WAS KEPT over the prisoners by two militia-men, a tall one named Chou and a shorter one named Ming. Living on the provisions seized and collected by the village elder, the two men guarded the village, watched over the growing crops, chased after runaway geese, and kept bandits at bay. They enforced the village rules and carried out the elder's wishes.

They had sipped from a jar of rice wine ear-lier to prepare themselves for the hanging and beheading tomorrow. After all, such was not an everyday occurrence. Their nerves needed stiffening.

Chou laid out three roughly carpentered coffins made of knotty pine planks. All was quiet, save for the elder's snoring and the occasional sniffling from the widow, who was standing on the stool. Buddha willing, she would doze off, slip off the stool, and hang herself to death before the destined time.

Some rats were making their rounds, sniffing around Miu Miu's and Tong Ting's bare toes as if they were sacrificial food. The village hall had long been the storage place for all seasonal grains seized and collected by the elder. Cats and rats abounded here.

At midnight, when the moon hid behind a thick cloud, Ming, the shorter of the two militiamen, was roused from sleep by the sound of shouting from the west end of the village, where the graveyard lay. He blinked his eyes and rubbed his ears to be certain that he had really heard the cries.

When the shouts came again, wrinkling the

silky darkness of the night, Ming hastened across the courtyard to stand at the front gate, which stood on high ground overlooking the entire village. There he not only heard the shouts again but saw someone carrying a torch running his way. "Ghost! Ghosts!" the man cried. "There are ghosts coming to our village. Stay indoors!"

It had to be the head monk, the only soul in the village unafraid of ghosts because of the sign of the zodiac tattooed on his palm: It was said to repel the dead and drive away ghosts.

The night watchman went back to wake his taller partner, who was snoozing and snoring rather loudly as he sat leaning against a column. "Wake up, Chou. Ghosts are coming!"

The guard snorted groggily. "What ghost?"

"The head monk from the temple is out there chasing ghosts!"

"Ghosts? From where?"

"The graveyard."

That snapped Chou wide-awake. "There aren't supposed to be ghosts running around before the killings. Only *after* the beheading, when the demons in hell claim their spirits. It's too soon, you fool." Yawning, he pushed his companion away. "Let me get some more sleep. Then you can take your turn."

"Ghosts!" came the shout again. This time it was loud and clear.

"Did you hear that?" Ming asked.

"Yes, I heard that." Chou grabbed his spear and stood up. "What shall we do? Are the ghosts coming our way?"

"They have to come our way. We have the dying right here."

"But we have to stand guard, no matter what," Chou said, looking nervously around the hall, dark in the dim moonlight.

"We should, shouldn't we?" Ming answered.

"You don't think we should?" Chou asked after a tense pause.

"You don't want to be in the path of a ghost, do you?"

Chou shot his short companion a hard stare. "Why not?"

"The ghosts might mistake us for the dead spirits and catch us instead, bringing us to the demons in hell."

"Stop it—you're scaring me."

"We shouldn't be scared by something like this, should we?" Ming said, his voice quavering.

"No, we shouldn't. We are the executioners of Goose Village. They should know us by now."

"Yeah, you're right," Ming said, trembling. "We are safe here together, you and I."

Suddenly the front gate was thrown open and in walked Master Wan, his torch flaming, his long robe trailing behind him. The monk looked at the two militiamen with his thick brows knit fiercely together. "Why didn't you latch the door? Didn't you hear me shouting?"

"Yes, but we didn't see any ghosts," Chou said.

"They are here early," the monk told him, swinging his torch over Miu Miu and Tong Ting. "I saw three ghosts fly out from the graveyard. I chased them away from unlatched doors, but lost them . . . wait . . . they are here."

"Look!" Ming cried out, shrinking back, pointing up. "I see something up there."

On the highest part of the gate wall stood a tall shadow, its bulbous head like a ferocious lion, its arms stretched out like the giant wings of an eagle. It walked slowly but steadily toward them. Letting out an eerie and haunting shriek, unlike any the guards had ever heard before, the ghost flew down at them, flapping its mighty wings.

The two guards dropped their spears and ran out of the front gate, not caring about their night duty or the pending executions. They screamed as the ghost shrieked again, and ran even faster. Chou tripped and fell. Ming ran on, heedless of his comrade's plight. Picking himself up, Chou ran after Ming toward the village proper until the night swallowed up their shadows and muted their footfalls.

Back in the ancestral hall, the winged ghost

took off his headgear: a lion's head used in the traditional lion dance each Spring Festival, borrowed from the temple. "What took you so long?" he asked Master Wan.

"I had to do my usual run from the graveyard," the monk replied.

Whipping out a dagger, the man sliced the ropes that fastened Miu Miu and Tong Ting, while the monk cut the rope from the widow's neck. They loaded the unconscious young couple into the carriage that was to have carried them to their beheading at sunrise.

"I didn't know you could play such a good ghost, Wu Ting," said Miu Miu's mother calmly as she seated herself inside the carriage.

"How did you know it was me?" Wu Ting asked, surprised. It was still too dark for her to see his features.

"No one in this village or the next is as tall as you," she answered. "I still remember when you used to bump your head against the top of our door frames when you apprenticed with us."

"It is an honor to be back at Goose Village," Wu Ting said, bowing.

"Goose Village . . . more like Devil Village. I hope they will pick another name someday. Thank you, Wu Ting. And you, too, Master Wan."

"My pleasure," the head monk replied. Putting a heavy lock on the front gate, he threw his torch over the wall into the hall, and placed the sheathed blue sword into the widow's arms. "Give this to Miu Miu," he said. "Not for war or battle, but for peace."

He whipped the mule, and the carriage moved forward. Behind them, the village hall caught fire and was soon engulfed in rising flames that reached from the wooden columns to the roof, spreading from the doorframes to the nearby trees.

Before them, a pensive Goose River lay waiting under a pale moon. A boat was anchored at the dock. One at a time, Wu Ting carried his young charges onto the boat. The boat wobbled and bobbed and sank down a few more inches when the monk helped the widow aboard. As soon as the lines were unfastened, the vessel floated into the middle of the stream, drawn slowly eastward by the current.

Standing on the dock, Master Wan bade the itinerants a silent good-bye with a bow, then drove his carriage unhurriedly back to his quiet temple, in time to begin another day of prayers at sunrise.

Hours later, when Miu Miu awoke on the rocking boat, she was surprised to see the vastness of the water surrounding her and the sun shining above. For a second she thought she had died and gone up to heaven. Then she saw her mother sitting next to her, and beside her a tall man rowing squeaky oars.

"Where am I?" Miu Miu asked.

"Shaanxi Lake," Mother answered.

"Why are we here?"

"Ask him—Tong Ting's father," her mother said, pointing at the rowing man. "After he tells you the tale, you have to pay him and

Monk Wan your respects. Our two families, Miu and Ting, have hope again. Clean up your groom," Mother said, gesturing to Tong Ting, who was still asleep near the stern. "We are going away. Far away from Goose Village. When we settle along the south shore of the lake, you and Tong Ting will be wed."

Lifting the blue sword, she threw it into the water. With barely a splash it sank down into the dark depths.

"Father's sword!" Miu Miu cried. "Why did you do that?"

"It's the only way to erase the last generation's bloodstain. I was wrong to send you on the path of revenge. A life shouldn't be repaid with death; it should only be rewarded with more lives to come. Have many children. Be prosperous. That will be your best gift to your father."

Miu Miu bowed deeply to her mother, then to her future father-in-law. With her fingers wrapped around the hand of her sleeping groom, Miu Miu looked toward the future, her eyes shining with tears that reflected a rising sun.

So begins a new life.

So ends the tale of a sword.

ACKNOWLEDGMENTS

Sunny, my ultimate chief editor, whose savviness and taste transcend my words, and whose love I live on and live for.

Victoria, a flower waiting to bloom. Shock the world with your wit.

Michael: Be the one you ought to be. Rise high, go far.

My mother: Your presence is love aplenty.

Mr. and Mrs. Liu: Your love is a river that never runs dry.

Special thanks to Nate and Mil, and their

lovely children—Austin Boston, Sammy Poughkeepsie, Erika the summer girl, and Hudson, whose life will be strong and long like the beloved river.

My esteemed writing group—John, Laura, Nina, Ron, Mary Louise, and Zach: Your artistry inspires me.

Alex Glass, a brilliant agent equipped with the most powerful weapon: fine taste.

Robert Gottlieb, the godfather to whom I'm indebted.

I am indebted to my very capable publicity manager, Cindy Tamasi, for her prodigious efforts to make this book known to all.

The editorial dream team of Christopher Caines, Renée Cafiero, and Jill Santopolo: You make the book shine.

Carla Weise, for a beautiful cover.

Laura Geringer: You are a visionary—the kind of brilliant editor all writers of the world ought to have but don't. I'm grateful for the seeds you planted in my mind. With your nurturing, we shall grow many a bountiful harvest together.